MARGARITA, I
that you enjoy reading
The Wing Man.

Tony Abruzzo is a retired Arizona lawyer who resides with his wife in Tucson. He has two daughters and three grandsons. He graduated from Dartmouth College and the University of Arizona College of Law. He served as an army sergeant in the infantry in Vietnam.

Tony Abruzzo

This novel was inspired by my friend Scott who nearly died as a result of a booby trap in Vietnam. Also by a disabled client who was murdered and left to die alone in the hot Arizona desert. Also, an unsolved double homicide in a small Arizona town and finally, by the defence of a young man suffering from traumatic brain injury who was falsely accused of serious crimes.

Tony Abruzzo

THE WING MAN

AUSTIN MACAULEY PUBLISHERS™

LONDON * CAMBRIDGE * NEW YORK * SHARJAH

Ordering Information
Quantity sales: Special discounts are available on quantity purchases by corporations, associations, and others. For details, contact the publisher at the address below.

Publisher's Cataloging-in-Publication data
Abruzzo, Tony
The Wing Man

ISBN 9781647509156 (Paperback)
ISBN 9781649791917 (ePub e-book)

Library of Congress Control Number: 2021920864

www.austinmacauley.com/us

First Published 2021
Austin Macauley Publishers LLC
40 Wall Street, 33rd Floor, Suite 3302
New York, NY 10005
USA

mail-usa@austinmacauley.com
+1 (646) 5125767

I acknowledge and thank the entire team at Austin Macauley, including Emma Jones, Production Coordinator, for their patience and expertise. I also thank Barbara Allen who helped format the Wing Man in the very early stages of my writing. Lastly, I acknowledge my wife who has supported me through thick and thin most of my adult years on Earth.

Chapter 1

Ben looked at the small white slip of paper with the name and phone number of Joe Harvey. It had slipped through his hand onto the carpet of his office. New client. Maybe a lot of money. As he stretched down to pick up the note, he felt it, a presence, energy, whatever it was, for the first time in many years. Not an eight-year-old boy taking care of his brother or a young soldier in Viet Nam any more. He was a lawyer, a husband, a father who needed to provide for his family. Something held him back from reaching the floor. He mumbled to himself and looked around the room.

"Leave me alone. Am I crazy, insane? Stay out of my life. Jesus, I'm talking to myself probably doesn't really exist. Who am I talking to? I must be schizophrenic. It's upset with me. I just know. It can't get its way all the time." His hand trembled as he picked up the elusive piece of paper and the phone.

Chapter 2

She walked through the door first. Biracial, half black/half Asian, small, very attractive. She smiled. Ben could not keep his eyes off her curvy, slender legs below the light-colored thin miniskirt. Tall, muscular, light brown skin, green eyes, the African-looking man was dressed like a cowboy, the boots, the hat, the whole outfit. The cordial chitchat at the beginning floated through the air haphazardly and vaporized on the way to Ben's ears. He again felt that something, a touch on his shoulder. Joe took off the cowboy hat.

"This is Lola, my fiancée. I have a business partner, an older lady… Let's call her the Dragon Lady. She's from South Korea, originally. Several years ago, we started a business venture. She put up the money. I did all the legwork, managed everything, did well. Now I'm stuck to face all the shit. It's all exaggerated crap! The so-called victims knew what they were doing and got paid for it."

His eyes bulged like the hawk that hung around Ben's backyard. Ben asked, "How did you get my name?"

"Stan Klein. He said that he could not represent me. Something about a conflict of interest. Here's the indictment."

Ben carefully read the several pages of charges. Lola's eyes focused on him, pierced his tightened chest. He rubbed the pained area, took a sip of his Diet Pepsi, and tried to hide his fear. Just forty years old, twelve years of practice, with only twenty criminal jury trials under his belt.

"Mr. Harvey, Joe, these kidnapping and sexual exploitation charges of the named young ladies could land you in prison for the rest of your life!"

"But, I didn't do half the shit on those papers. Whose side are you on?"

"I'm just saying how serious they are. To be honest, I've never represented anyone facing life in prison. Nothing like this. Maybe you should talk to an older attorney, more experienced, someone who has had similar cases before."

Ben's shoulders loosened, felt free.

"No, no. I've known Stan for several years, and I trust him. He referred me to you, has confidence in you. You're my man. Listen, money is no problem. I can get $50,000.00 by tomorrow to start."

When Ben heard the number, his eyes expanded, and his crotch area tightened, creating a strange feeling of pain and delight. Shoulder spasms up the side of his neck began. He managed to stand up, attempting to reject the physical pressure. He wanted to be independent, his own man. He blurted the words, "OK, I'll do it." He reached into his file cabinet and wrote a few words on a long piece of paper. "Here's the contract. Read it. Take it with you. Bring it back to me signed and with the retainer. Then I'll start working for you."

Ben stuck his hand out. Strong, sinewy fingers surrounded and engulfed his hand. He suddenly felt cold, alone, with an emptiness in his gut, but also liberated. Opposite forces compressed together like the chocolate and cream of an Oreo cookie.

Chapter 3

Prosecutor Delores Huerta, Lori to her friends, was the same person she had always been. Condescending and exuding moral superiority. Ben unsuccessfully tried to date her in law school. Her jet-black hair, pure white skin, shapely legs, and concave lips also had not changed much over the last decade or so.

"Ben, you've turned into a real whore, willing to represent anyone as long as you're getting paid. Your client, Joe Harvey, or whatever his real name is, is a scumbag, not worthy to be part of the human race!"

"Wait a minute, Lori. Everyone's entitled to a competent defense. Anyway, he says that the charges are bogus, exaggerated, not true."

Her large brown eyes became laser beams cutting right through him.

"Don't ever call me Lori again! Innocent? Are you shitting me? This asshole held ten teenage Asian girls captive for over a year. Forced them into prostitution. Threatened them by saying he would turn them over to immigration. He and some woman, whereabouts unknown, set the whole thing up. They kidnapped girls from Thailand, the Philippines, even Viet Nam! The girls were told that they only had to give massages. Massages, my ass! Four of the girls became pregnant. One almost bled to death from an ectopic complication. Only fifteen years old. Thank goodness that a kind nurse from Thailand reached out and spoke to her. The whole massage scam collapsed after that. Your client is a monster who will spend the rest of his miserable life behind bars!"

Ben stood up. He felt like a rat caught in a trap with a chunk of cheese in his mouth.

"Listen, I'll do some investigation and get back to you. Maybe I can find this other person that you're talking about and clear things up. Are any of your ladies willing to speak to me for interviews? I want to do a thorough job."

"Dream on, Ben. You know the rules. The girls have no desire to be interviewed by you. Read the police reports and medical records. They clearly show the evil your client has engaged in. As to the other perpetrator, my office will always be interested in any information you have to offer, but even if you help us get this other person convicted, your client would still be looking at mucho years behind bars."

Ben smiled. "I love it when you speak Spanish. It reminds me of law school. Remember when we drank a few beers and I asked you to teach me Spanish?"

She looked at him and laughed. "You were unsuccessful then with your bullshit, and you will suffer the same reality now."

He rushed to the door. "It was nice talking to you, Delores."

Chapter 4

Ben sweated when he reviewed the photos, police reports, and hospital records. They were frightful to look at, even for a Viet Nam veteran who had seen the bloody remains of soldiers' limbs. The deep scars on the girls' bodies evidenced the torture and punishment they were forced to endure. But the faces! The desperation, fear, sadness, and resignation in their eyes caused him to turn around and look at the pictures of his wife and children on the wall behind his desk. Smiling, happy faces. Did these young ladies have anything to smile about? Insecurity and doubt crept in.

"Should I have taken this case? Am I the whore the prosecutor accused me of being? Do I have the balls to face a jury?" The shades were drawn in his office as he agonized over the evidence of misery and tragedy before him. The phone rang.

"Are you eating with us tonight? It is almost seven o'clock."

He softly answered in the affirmative and ran to his parked eight-year-old red Ford Granada.

Chapter 5

Stan Klein, a tall, thin, balding sixty-nine-year-old criminal defense attorney with more than two hundred jury trials under his belt over his forty years of practice, was tired. A long day. Time to go home. He would relax, drink some good scotch, and eat sardines and crackers in his expensive town house in the exclusive gated community. After starting the engine of his new, shiny, black Cadillac DeVille, he blankly stared in his rearview mirror and thought about what he had set in motion.

"Why did I refer this animal to Ben? What was I thinking? Never thought he would actually get hired. I just wanted to get him out of my office… Jesus Christ!"

He pounded the dashboard. No, scotch alone would not be enough to get him through the night. He directed the Cadillac to the apartment he rented for his new young squeeze, a thirty-year-old divorced blonde with an hourglass figure, a pretty face, and a mind filled with worms and snakes that never stopped squirming.

Chapter 6

"Ben, that bitchy prosecutor, Delores, is on the phone. She was nasty to me. Wanted to know if you had yet crawled into the office."

"I got it. Don't worry about her. She just has her moods."

"Good morning, Delores."

"I can't believe it. One of the girls is willing to talk to you. She calls herself Candy. Her real name is too hard to pronounce. Viet Namese, fifteen years old."

"Just curious. Why is she agreeable to the interview?"

"Even with the shit she's been through, Candy's not bitter, but grateful to be alive. She asked me about you. I told her you served in the Army in Viet Nam. She was impressed with that. Her mom always told her that the GIs were nice to the Viet Namese women. The mother talked about getting candy, cigarettes, stuff like that. Anyway, I'll call you when I set up the meeting."

"*Hasta la proxima*," came out of Ben's mouth. He was proud that he could speak Spanish to his adversary.

He heard a quiet reply. "*Lo mismo a usted, hombre.*"

Chapter 7

Ben could not sleep. The same thoughts over and over. Was he on a collision course with his loyal, silent, elusive, vaporous friend who had always protected him? But now? Was this situation different?

His mind wandered to a day in Brooklyn when he was eight years old. His mother asked him to hold on to the stroller carrying his six-month-old brother. Only for a short while, she entered the store, picked up the item waiting for her, and returned. Some wires in his brain must have crossed causing a short circuit. His body pushed the stroller toward the street. He visualized the event in slow motion as if it occurred yesterday. Both of his hands held tightly on to the stroller. The noise of the speeding cars got louder and louder. Why was he doing this? Had some energy or power taken over? He suddenly felt two hands covering his. The direction of the stroller changed, and it collided with a parking meter stopping its progress. Ben heard a high-pitched scream.

"What were you doing? Were you trying to hurt your brother?"

His mother grabbed the infant in her arms and looked at Ben as she had never before. Fear, bewilderment, confusion. They slowly and silently walked home. No words were ever spoken about the incident by anyone.

Chapter 8

"Hello, Joe, Ben, your lawyer. I've reviewed the police reports, photos, and medical records. Does not look good for you. Ten girls are scheduled to testify against you. Only one is willing to be interviewed."

Joe yelled over the phone. "Which one?"

"Candy, a Viet Namese girl."

"That slut bitch. She told me that she was eighteen. How the fuck could I know she was younger? She gave Johns blow jobs at $50.00 a pop. My manager only found out when she caught her in the act."

"What manager? Who is she? I need to talk to her."

"You met her already. Lola. The sexy one with the short skirt in the office. No need to interview Lola yet. First, find out what that liar Candy says. Make sure I get a copy of everything. I'll pick up the papers tomorrow, whenever I can get down there."

"Joe, the photos look bad. Who did all the damage to the girls? Looks like they were tortured." Ben heard a scream, a bellowing through the phone.

"You're not fucking listening to me! I didn't know about the sex or anything else! I'll be there sometime tomorrow."

Ben heard the click. He shook his head, peered out the window, and prayed that the gusty wind and radiant blue sky held some answers to the emerging puzzle.

Chapter 9

Jennifer screamed as she stood over him. "Ben, come to bed. You fell asleep again on the couch. Almost midnight. I can't sleep with your snoring. Put on your mask."

"Sure, sure, I'll be right there."

He knew that the short walk to the bedroom would wake him out of his delirium and cause him to stare at the ceiling for hours while his wife would gently breathe next to him. He was right. His mind wandered. Another flashback. Cu Chi, Viet Nam, 1970. Sgt. Ben Russo, in the country for two weeks, woke up from a sound sleep on a rice paddy with thick, painful, swollen lips.

"Those fucking mosquitos got me again. I'll kill that water rat if it gets any closer. I'll chop that disgusting tail into pieces!"

Lt. Russell yelled. "Russo, Bennett was taken back to base camp early this morning. He's got the runs, probably dysentery. The dumb fuck drank water from the barrel in the hooch we raided last night. He didn't know that's where they cleaned their clothes. You're stuck carrying the ammo for the M60 with Donovan. We're leaving in ten minutes. You better go now."

The rays of the sun slithered through the small openings of the bamboo shoots in the thick jungle. Just enough light to give warning of the snakes and marauding red ants on the wet, muddy ground. After humping for several hours, they saw a ridge, one hundred yards wide, almost east and west, on higher ground. The Lieutenant barked.

"We'll set up on the ridge for the night. I want the machine guns to pull security on the east and west ends. Donovan, move to one of the sides."

Donovan's Irish face and freckles blended into one red, circular blob.

"Go Russo, left or right. Let's do it."

As Ben started to go to the left, some thing or force unseen, attached to his left shoulder, pushed him to the right. He did not have the energy to resist. He trudged to the right side carrying fifty pounds of gear, M60 ammo, and an M16 rifle. As he laid down the machine gun rounds on the ground, a mind-jostling roar caused his ears to ring. His eyes and nose burned from the smoke. He heard moaning, groaning, screams. He ran toward the sounds. The Lieutenant stopped him.

"Stay back! Stay back! Four men are down. I'm calling in a medevac. Pull security."

Donovan in a hushed tone asked Ben the following morning. "Ben, how did you know which side not to go? A booby trap. I heard that two guys lost a leg, one guy an arm, and Truman, a leg and one eye. Man, are you religious or are we just fucking lucky?"

Ben brushed off the mud, opened his canned food, and was silent for a few seconds. "You know, Mike, if I told you, you wouldn't believe me. Let's just hope it continues."

"OK, Russo, don't lose it or fuck it up. I only have four more months in this shithole."

Ben woke up because of the tugging on his arm. Jennifer again.

"Why do you talk in your sleep and toss and turn so much? I'm going to sleep with the girls if you keep doing this!"

"Yeah, yeah, all right. I'll be quiet now." He turned away and mumbled. "At least I'm here. Scott didn't get that chance."

Jennifer rose up. "What did you say?"

"Nothing."

Chapter 10

"Candy, this is Mr. Ben Russo. He is the lawyer representing Joe Harvey. He is here to interview you. Remember, any time you want to stop talking, that is OK. You can go at any time. Do you understand everything I've told you?"

Ben stared at the shy, beautiful young lady who fidgeted with her long brown hair and stared at the floor. Her high cheekbones and almond-shaped eyes looked Asian, but the lighter hair, white skin, and taller frame reminded him of the French/Viet Namese girls he had seen in the country. She looked sturdy, with wide hips and shoulders. As her face rose, her smile showed a few shiny gold teeth in the front.

"Hello, Mr. Russo."

"Candy, I am so happy to meet you. I have read all your statements, seen the photos… I am so sorry for that."

She touched the lower part of her neck and the dark, disfigured thick skin not concealed by her blouse.

Ben placed a few photos before her. "I know that this may be hard for you to explain. Please tell me how you suffered the marks on your throat, back of your thighs, and back."

Candy's eyes narrowed as she spoke without hesitation. "The man placed the iron poker into the fire. I was handcuffed behind my back. My feet were roped together. Two women held me down. The poker was placed on my skin. I screamed as loud as I could. I smelled the skin burning. The women laughed. The man had on a mask and said nothing."

Ben softly asked, "Why did they do this to you?"

Candy jumped up from her chair and with both hands over her mouth shrieked, "I was a virgin! I am a virgin! I would not give that up, for just anyone. Their orders meant nothing to me. They could not force me to become a used woman." She sobbed. The prosecutor put her arms around her.

"Do you still want to talk?"

She nodded up and down. Delores looked at Ben.

"Let's take a break. Come back in ten minutes." He entered the adjoining room and stared at the copious outline he had prepared for the interview. "Fuck those questions. I'll do this my way."

The prosecutor sat closer to Candy than before. Ben focused on the young eyes. "Tell me how you traveled from Viet Nam to the United States. Take your time. I will not interrupt you."

"The first thing I remember was living in Cu Chi with my mother and her family. I had no father. When I asked her why, she would only cry. No Americans were there. Only Viet Namese soldiers. We worked on a farm, on the rice paddies, in the hot sun. The rain in the afternoon cooled us down. We were poor but had enough to eat. One day, some soldiers came and took me and my mom away. We cried, screamed, asked why. They laughed and called us a lot of mean names. When my uncles tried to stop them, they beat them with their rifles. We were taken to a bad place, where we had to work all day with little food. Had to sleep on the hard ground. I was there until I was eleven years old."

Delores placed her hand on Candy's shoulder. "Ben, Candy was put into a reeducation camp for people who the government believed were American sympathizers. The camps were dreadful but served the purpose of free labor for the government."

Candy looked up. "Our lives were no good. My mom had to sweep the fields for bombs, booby traps, left by the Viet Cong. She stepped on one. Blown up into pieces. The soldiers smiled when they showed her bloody pieces to me. They called her bad names, put her in a bag, dumped her into a hole, and burned her. They forced me to watch. I will never forget the flames."

She placed her head between her legs and remained silent. Delores caressed her back.

He asked, "Candy, how did you escape, get out of the camp?"

Her eyes lit up. Her hands balled up into fists. "After they burned my mother, there was nothing there for me to stay. A few of us young people stayed up for nights thinking of how we could leave. There was one male guard on duty at night who was supposed to watch us. One of the girls with us received extra food from him, almost every night. We forced her to tell us why."

Her hands now showed her white knuckles. "She was a traitor, told him everything we talked about. He gave her candy, soap, sweets…even meat when he could. We told her to take his hand, go into the deep bushes, and satisfy him, keep him busy. She asked why. We said that if she did not, we would tell the commander what the soldier had given her. He was cruel, would beat her, maybe even kill her in front of everybody, as an example." She sipped some water from the glass in front of her and stared at both of them. "That night, after hearing their sounds in the bushes, we six escaped. It was easy. The fence was low, and there was little moonlight. Four boys, two girls. We traveled at night and slept in the forest during the day. The rivers and streams provided us with water and food. Only one problem in Cambodia. But we made it through."

Ben stuck his chin out. "Your group traveled through Cambodia without the Khmer Rouge catching you, killing you?"

She showed some teeth, then became sad. "One of us died. Chou got caught swimming. We heard the soldiers talking and the gunshots and ran away. They never found us. We were more careful after that. It took eight weeks to get to Bangkok."

Delores asked, "How did you survive? Did you have friends there?"

Candy shrugged her shoulders. "There were others from Viet Nam who had escaped. Some by foot, others by boat." Her eyes watered. "For two years, these people helped me, loved me, enabled me to stay alive. I will never forget them."

She blew her nose with the handkerchief Delores handed her.

"When I was thirteen, everybody said that I was pretty. I spoke a little English because of my mom. I needed money, work. I got a job as a waitress, then a dancer, in a nice bar. Men from many countries were there to drink, meet women, even pay for sex. I always said no. I was still very young and spoke to them nicely. Nobody forced me. They clapped when I danced on the pole to the American rock and roll music. Things were OK. The owners of the bar let us keep some of the tips. I made enough money to live with a few other dancers in a small apartment and for food. If they caught us hiding any of the money, they would beat us. If we got bruises and could not dance until they healed, that made them even madder."

Delores spoke. "It is getting late. You look tired, Candy. Do you want to go on or come back another day?"

"No, it makes me feel better to tell you what happened to me and the other girls."

Ben said, "You are a brave, young lady."

Candy momentarily smiled. "One day, the owners introduced us to a man and a woman from America. Their names are Joe and… Lola?" She looked toward the prosecutor who nodded. "I understood what they were saying. Six girls were there. They said that if we went to America and danced in the bars there, we would each get an apartment to live in, keep half of our tips, and have one day a week off to rest. They seemed nice. We believed them. We signed some papers and a month later were put on a large boat with many other girls. We got on during the night and had to stay hidden in the bottom of the boat. Very little food and water. The bathroom only at night. We were scared. The men on the boat said that some would get off in Hawaii and others later in Los Angeles." Candy finished the glass of water with one gulp. "I stayed on the boat for three weeks. They let us out in California. Five of us in an apartment with three beds, a bathroom, and a small kitchen. I danced for one year…no sex. Then Joe and Lola came to the bar and told us that we were going to Tucson to learn how to be masseuses. That we would massage men for bigger money than we were getting for dancing. We asked if we had to do anything else. Lola said that we would talk about that later. Joe gave her an angry look when she said that."

Ben asked, "Tell us about Tucson, Candy."

"In the beginning, everything was OK. They taught us how to do massages. Every day, I did at least ten. But then Lola talked to each of us and demanded more."

Delores asked, "What did she say?"

"Lola was nice in the beginning. She asked me if I would be willing to have sex with the customers, if they asked. That would make them happier and I would make a lot more money. I said no. She went away. A week later, she asked again. I said no. She called a man in the room. A big man, he wore a mask. She held me down. He beat me with a belt. He stopped when my blood soaked the belt."

Delores intervened. "How many times did this happen to you?"

"Three times. After the last time, I told Lola I would do it. I lied. I was a virgin and wanted to be a virgin when I got married. I did not want to get pregnant. I knew what I had to do."

24

Ben asked, "What was that?"

"The men liked me. They said how pretty I was. I spoke nice to them in English. When my hands went over their bodies, many wanted more. I told them how young I was. Still, some did not care. I did not want another beating from the man in the mask. I bought condoms, forced myself to do oral sex on them.

"Almost all were satisfied. Only a few demanded more. When that happened, I cried. They would get nervous and leave the room."

Delores asked, "What about Lola? Did she complain to you?"

"No, she said that I could do what I was doing. Only because I serviced more men than the others. I was the most popular girl. She even gave me more money than the others. Told me not to say anything to the girls or to Joe if he ever came in."

The prosecutor stood up. "Ben, Candy has told us the essence of her future testimony. Do you have anything else?"

Ben put his pad down. "Just a few questions. Candy, did you ever see Joe at the massage parlor? Did he ever beat you?"

"No, Mr. Russo, I never saw him."

He haltingly asked, "You said that you were beaten with a belt? Did it leave any scars on you?"

Before Delores had a chance to stop her, Candy turned around and pulled down the back of her pants, showing her naked buttocks to all. The scar tissue was long. Looked like a flagpole in design. Ben momentarily looked and then put his head down and closed his eyes. Delores muttered and shook her head.

"What monsters!" She turned to Ben. "Ben, after hearing Candy today, this Lola lady will be arrested and indicted for the same charges as your client. Let's go, Candy, we're done here."

Candy sobbed in her hands. Delores rubbed her shoulder. "What's the matter, sweetie?"

Candy raised her head. "I miss my momma, my Mona."

Delores asked, "Was that your mother's name?"

"She told me that the Americans gave her that name."

Ben's throat dried up as he spoke. "Did you say, Mona?"

"Yes, Mr. Russo."

Chapter 11

Ben was surprised and annoyed when Lola, instead of Joe, entered his office unannounced to pick up the paperwork. She ignored the secretary and walked like a cheetah after devouring its prey.

"Lola, I did not expect you. Where's Joe?"

"Ben, you are going to find out that nothing happens without me knowing about it. He and I are partners, attached at the hip, if you know what I mean."

Ben stared at her smile and teeth that were so shiny and white. He knew that only an acid job by a dentist could produce such splendor. He mentally pivoted to the case at hand. "Because of yesterday's interview with a former employee of yours, you also have the same problems Joe has. The prosecutor told me that you are going to be arrested and indicted."

"Fuck her and the lying snitch you talked to. These girls are all a bunch of bitches and whores…ungrateful…deserved all they got."

Ben sensed that this lady wanted to talk. If he were patient and polite, she would give him more information than he would ever get from Joe's mouth. He needed to be subtle, careful, not too eager. He forced a smile and nodded.

"Lola, here's the paperwork to hand over to Joe to review." He got up from behind his desk and handed her a large brown envelope. "But if you want to talk, give me your side of the story. We can do it now. I have the time. I'm technically only Joe's attorney but since you two are two peas in a pod, I'll consider whatever you tell me as attorney-client privilege…you know, confidential."

"Two peas in a pod? What the hell are you talking about?"

Ben smiled. "Like you said—partners."

She sat down, crossed her legs, and deeply breathed as she paused. "OK, attorney Russo, this is the truth. These bitches were never forced to do anything they didn't agree to first. They lied about their ages and everything else. Joe and I never laid a hand on them." She looked at him to make sure he was paying attention.

"Sure, Lola, I'm listening. Tell me more. Keep talking."

And talking she did, for almost two hours. Ben hid his excitement by pretending to yawn and stared at his watch on several occasions. That only motivated her more, to spill all the beans, show him how important she was. He nodded, winked, shook his head, empathized. She gave up almost everything about the organization, even mentioned the Dragon Lady once. He hesitantly asked. "So, this lady, the one in charge, does she have a real name?"

Lola's face winced. She raised her chin in an effort to stretch her tightened neck muscles. The transparent expression on her face changed into a lifeless, stationary mold. She said nothing. He needed to get back on track, but his body language was awkward, not in sync. Still he persisted.

"Oh, come on Lola, what's her name? This is just between you and me. She's probably out of the country, anyway."

She stood up and pushed her finger into his chest. "Ask your buddy, Stan. He knows who she is."

She hustled out of the office and slammed the door.

Chapter 12

After a sleepless night of tossing and turning, Ben gave up any hope of real sleep and began to daydream of his younger days. He enjoyed going down memory lane. Life was so much simpler then, with fewer nuances to clog up your mind. He had felt so free up until the time of graduating college with his B.A. in English. But then his parents asked, "Are you going to teach English in high school?"

The thought of teaching Frost, Thoreau, Emerson, or Hemingway to testosterone-laden boys and love-struck girls frightened him, depressed him.

"Did I waste four years of my life reading Shakespeare, *The Canterbury Tales* in Middle English? What the hell was I thinking? I'm not prepared for anything. Now I have to worry about getting killed in Viet Nam?"

Most of his college friends had a plan. Join ROTC in the last semester. Make believe you wanted to be an officer and drag out the training as long as you could. Get a doctor, any quack would do, to fill out a form that said you had bad knees, bad joints, bad asthma, bad freaking anything to get you out of the draft. A friend even gave him the name of a doctor who helped him get 4F status. Instead, he just hung around his parents' house for a few months, vegged out, and spent his time trying to screw as many women as he could. He knew that another phase of his life was about to begin. And soon it did with horrific force and pain. From the first day, the training sergeants were on his ass.

"So, you're a college boy? You couldn't figure out a way to get out of this man's army? Go down and give me twenty pushups. Show me that you're not a weak, fat, stupid fuck!"

Everyone and everything from the recruiting station, basic training, and infantry training seemed so surreal, so bizarre, so foreign, except for one friendship he maintained throughout, even into Viet Nam. A young recruit on the second day stuck out his hand. "Ben, my name's Scott, Scott Berkman. I saw the sergeant get on you yesterday. This place is…interesting."

Ben soon found out that this guy was different. A college grad with no chip on his shoulder, not overly concerned with his imminent future, and always with a Jerry Lewis side to him. "Scott, you didn't even try to get out of this shit, did you?"

"You know, Ben, I majored in accounting and economics because my dad wanted me to join his business, become his partner. He owns the biggest Buick dealership on Long Island. Makes a ton of money. But I don't want to sell Buick Rivieras for the rest of my life."

Ben smiled. "So how did you wind up here?"

"I knew that I wanted to do something different from everyone in my family. The same routine. Work at the dealership, follow the rules, make good money, marry a nice, rich Jewish girl, have kids, and on and on. But when my dad sent me to a doctor for a so-called checkup that was the proverbial nail in the coffin. The doctor told me that I had flat feet, bad ankles, bad knees, and asthma. He said that I was unfit for military service that I'd never make it through basic training. He was going to sign a form that would get me classified as 4F."

Ben's ears perked up.

"So, what screwed up the plan?"

Scott looked at him squarely in his eyes. "Plan? That was not my plan. I played football, baseball, and wrestled in high school. Rugby in college. There was nothing wrong with me. But that wasn't the issue."

Ben made a face. "What issue?"

"Well, at least my issue. I read the papers. Look around here. You know why they're giving you and me such a hard time? What about one hundred guys here, mostly black and Puerto Rican? Only two college graduates in the whole group? You and me."

Ben asked, "So what does that mean? Who cares?"

"Listen, Ben, I'm no hero, no do-gooder, but this government is fighting a war with poor white, black, and Puerto Rican guys with no education or future. That sucks. Not right. If these poor slobs have to go, I'm going with them." He looked at Ben. "I guess you must think I'm crazy?"

Ben laughed. "Not crazy, just fucked up, like me. No direction, nowhere to go, all dressed up without a date…"

"Hold up, Ben. No more clichés. We're stuck here. Let's make the best of it and get out of this man's army without getting our balls blown off."

Ben had to ask, "By the way, what did your parents say when you walked out of the doctor's office?"

Scott grimaced. "They haven't spoken to me since that day. They know that I'm here. But they'll cry when I get shipped over to Nam. They still love me."

Ben's eyes widened. "How do you know they'll send us there?"

"Come on, Ben, you see the college demonstrators causing trouble, giving the finger to the government. They want to send us. Have to. Revenge. Payback time. Pay the fiddler."

Ben grinned. "Now who's into clichés?"

He always smiled when he thought of Scott. It gave him a peaceful feeling. Not necessary now to ruin the moment and go deeper down memory lane. Maybe at a later time. He fell into a deep sleep on the sofa with newspapers and magazines on his chest.

Chapter 13

When he woke up, he tried to suppress the urge to dig deeper into the inevitable hole he was creating for himself. His psyche was in gear. Too many similarities. Cu Chi. Scott. Candy. Mona. One voice demanded that he not turn over any more rocks. Nothing good could come out of it. The other voice wanted to know more, to learn the absolute truth, no matter the consequences, in order to make it right.

He arrived earlier than usual at the office. At 8 am, the prosecutor's receptionist put him on hold.

"Hello, Delores Huerta speaking."

He spoke almost in a whisper. "Ben Russo here. You're going to hate me for asking…"

"Come on, Ben, I have a hearing in thirty minutes. Speak fast."

"I need a few more minutes with Candy. Just a couple of questions I forgot to ask. It will take no more than ten minutes."

"Can't you just write the questions down and I'll call you back with the answers?"

"No, you'll realize later why it has to be in person."

"This is my last favor. Talk to you later."

Ben opened the brown envelope that contained all of his Viet Nam memorabilia, commendations, and awards. He remembered his last conversation with his friend in Cu Chi.

"Scott, that young woman who cleans up the hooch stares at you all the time. I think she likes you."

"Ben, you and I have been together since the beginning of this ordeal. We're short, thank God, close to the end. Nothing bad yet. Knock on wood. I want to tell you something you need to keep to yourself. A secret."

Ben squinted. "No need to tell me anything. What happens in Viet Nam stays here."

31

Scott shook his head. "No, this is important to me. I'm not asking for your approval. I just need to get it out of me, tell it to somebody I care about. Do you understand?"

"This sounds serious. Go ahead."

"You know the photo machine near the chow hall? Look at these."

Ben glanced at the three small photos of Scott smiling next to a Viet Namese woman and handed them back. "Why did you take pictures of you and the cleaning lady together? What's going on?"

"You're going to think I'm crazy. My parents are going to kill me, disown me. I really like this girl, maybe even…love her. We've been together many times. I'm thinking about marrying her, bring her back to the U.S. after my tour ends in two months."

Ben stood up and shouted. "Are you fucking out of your mind? You're just lonely—

"Horny—not thinking straight. Your dick has taken over your brain! Don't even try to do this. The Army probably won't let you anyway." He put his arm on his best friend's shoulder. "Listen, when you get back to New York and get to screw those big-breasted Jewish girls waiting for a guy like you, you'll forget this…lady. What's her name anyway?"

Scott giggled, smiled. "I gave her a name. Don't laugh. Her real name is too long, hard to pronounce. When we make love, and not screw like you described it, she moans so sweetly… I nicknamed her Mona because of that. She has no idea why I picked that name."

Ben got closer, in his face. "You're my only real friend here. Don't ruin your life. Don't let it happen. Have you told her your plan yet?"

Scott stood back a few steps. "I'll do that in a few days. I agreed to help a newbie on a recon mission with a sniper who is also new. The old sniper will go too. He's leaving the country in two weeks, has to train the other guy. The sergeant asked me—thought that the new guys needed someone to be with them, just in case. We're not going out very far. Anyway, keep it to yourself, what I told you. Here, keep one set of these photos for a memento. Catch you later. I'm going to bed, have to leave at four in the morning."

Ben, the attorney, cried. His tears fell on the two photos he held in his hands. That was the last time he saw his friend. The V.C. had wired a U.S. artillery round into a supersized booby trap. The explosion killed all four when the new sniper stepped on a bed of leaves on the trail. He sobbed as he kissed his friend's photo.

"I love you, Scott—will never forget you."

He placed his head between his arms on the desk. He picked up the ringing phone.

"Delores Huerta is on the line."

"Ben, Candy liked you. She agreed to talk to you again. Be in my office today at four. Remember, only ten minutes. See you then."

Chapter 14

For the next several hours, hysteria, fear, panic, and delusionary thoughts took over. Ben could not eat. But he had to have a drink—several of them from the bottle hidden in his office. He told his secretary to cancel all his appointments and to go home for the day. He wanted to be alone. After three Irish whiskeys, he dozed off. The phone rang. His body was drenched with sweat.

"Ben, Delores. Candy got here early. Can you come over now?"

He splashed water on his red, moistened face in the bathroom, and held the small envelope in his hand as tightly as he would handle a hand grenade. He did not nod or speak to anyone as he walked, punched the button of the elevator, and traveled the six levels above. It felt like glue was between his lips. He could not open his mouth. Delores wondered why his face was so red, so puffy.

"OK, Ben, we're ready."

He managed to cope with his dizziness and sat on a chair opposite the two ladies.

"Candy, I served in Viet Nam. You already know that. I spent five months of my tour in Cu Chi."

Candy sat up higher in her chair.

"I had a very close friend, Army friend. His name was Scott. I can show you his picture."

Delores spoke up. "Come on, Ben, what's this all about? Don't waste our time."

"Please… I'm doing the best I can. Here…look at this."

Candy glanced at the photo.

"This friend, Scott, had a friend in Cu Chi…a young lady. Do you want to see her picture?" His hand trembled. After she nodded, he placed the photo before her. "You can pick it up."

As she held it in her hand, Delores looked over her shoulder. Candy teared up, kissed the photo, and held it close to her chest.

Delores grabbed his tie. "What are you pulling here? Who is this woman? Are you trying to scare Candy?"

Ben put both of his hands over his wet eyes and softly spoke. "Candy, I know that the picture is of your mom, Mona. The man, Scott, in the other photo, is your dad. He died a few days after they were taken. He loved your mother…wanted to marry her. He was my best friend. His parents may still be alive. I wanted you to know all of this. The photos are yours to keep, if you want them."

Candy raised her eyes, stared at the photos again, and hugged Delores and Ben, sobbing on their shoulders.

Delores made sure that Candy left with a police escort. Ben sat on his chair staring at the floor. She spoke through her red, soggy eyes.

"What are you going to do, Ben? You technically have no conflict of interest. You need to tell your client everything that happened today. You will still be his attorney, if he objects."

He stood up and sighed. "I don't care what he says. I'm getting out."

Delores hesitated, then touched his shoulder. "Just so you know, I believe that you are an honorable man. The other ladies are scared, do not want to testify."

"Candy's my best witness, maybe my only witness. We have a complicated situation."

Ben slowly walked to the door. "I'll talk to you soon. Pray for me."

She smiled. "You're going to need all the help you can get, amigo."

Chapter 15

Joe's eyes revealed a deep, cold, lifeless hate. "Are you fucking kidding me? You are quitting as my attorney because you knew the guy screwing this slut's mother? In Viet Nam? I paid you a lot of money. More is on the way. Do you have shit for brains? That dumb bitch Lola told you too much!"

Ben briefly closed his eyes and looked toward the ceiling of his darkened office. They were alone. He had to be careful with his words.

"Joe, you do not want me as your attorney. I know too much. Lola got on a roll, had diarrhea of the mouth. The main witness against you is the daughter of a friend I loved. You have to understand."

Joe ripped up the letter he had received from Ben. "Love? Remember the person I mentioned to you? I called her the Dragon Lady?" He walked over to the window. The sun was beginning to set. He turned around. "You know, Ben, you don't seem like that bad of a guy. More decent than the other scumbag lawyers that I've met. And you're probably a good trial attorney. Stan said you would fight for us, not judge us for what we've done. But the big thing that he told us was that we'd be able to trust you because of your loyalty and dedication to your clients. That's total bullshit! You don't give a fuck about me or Lola, who just got served with the arraignment notice."

He put his bloodshot eyes close to Ben's face. The spittle from his mouth sprayed as he shouted and grabbed his lawyer's shirt. "Do you know who'll be dead soon if you are allowed to abandon me with the knowledge of the organization in your head? Me, you clueless bastard!"

He wiped his face and mouth with the sleeve of his shirt. "I am nothing, just one local man, part of an international organization making millions of dollars each year. Do you think she is going to let a dipshit like you ruin her business, send people she needs to prison?"

Ben stared at Joe's disheveled face. Almost felt sorry for him. Joe walked around the room as he spoke.

"I put my life on the line in Viet Nam, here, and in Thailand. I met the right people in Bangkok on my R&R. The way the soldiers stared at the girls when they danced. The pleasure they received when they fucked these young, hairless beauties. I know, I did. Big money could be made if you put it together, organized it. Are you listening? I've paid my dues. I went back after my duty with the 101st Airborne was completed. As soon as my government let me."

He sat down, looked toward the window. "I hooked up with my old Thai buddies. But an idea without money is like a fart—it comes and goes. That's when the Dragon Lady came in with the money, global connections, planning. She is brilliant, part of a rich, cultured family, someone who does not want to be exposed by a dumb prick like you!"

Ben was now scared. The expression on Joe's face was not human. He had to try something and quick.

"Listen, what you and Lola told me is confidential, attorney-client privilege. Nobody else will ever know. You're safe. I'll just tell the Judge that you and I had a falling out—you know—our relationship has soured. We've lost trust in one another. The Judge will not care, especially if the prosecutor does not object."

Joe got up, grabbed the two framed photos of Ben's daughters on his desk—ten and twelve years old. They smiled, beamed for the camera, looked so happy. His finger touched the face of each girl.

"You know, they are about the same age most of our girls begin their training. We go real slow, carefully process and program their minds, personalities, as their bodies grow into money-making luscious fruits." He gently placed the frames back where he found them and turned to Ben. "They look like solid candidates, perfect. You'll never find them. But even if you got lucky and did, they won't be the same little angels and darlings they once were. Do you understand what I just said?"

Ben stood up, pointed toward the door. "Get your sleazy, oily body out of my sight. I warn you now. If you argue to the Judge against my removal, I will tell him that you threatened to kidnap my daughters and exploit them in your godless world. Get the fuck out of my office!"

Joe stared at Ben in disbelief, like a large snake would, if attacked by a mouse.

"You mentioned God? I doubt that He exists. But if He does, that's the only thing that could save your precious girls from becoming two wet pink holes filled up with the sperm of strangers! See you in court."

He sauntered out of the office and never looked back.

Ben attacked the door to the credenza and grabbed the half-full bottle of Bushmills. He did not even use a glass.

Chapter 16

The day had finally come. As he rushed up the steps to the courthouse, he heard a voice behind him.

"Ben, stop. I have to talk to you."

Stan Klein's bald head was wet with large droplets of sweat. The bags under his eyes were dark red, almost purple. The blood vessels on his bulbous nose looked like they were about to explode. He put his hands together as if he were about to either pray or beg.

"Are you crazy? Have you lost any sense of reason? Do you know what you are doing? Please wait." Stan reached up and grabbed Ben by the collar with both hands. "Why are you betraying me? You do not know the people you are dealing with. It may be too late for me. Stay in the case. Do it for your wife, family, daughters—if you don't give a shit about me."

The anguished expression tempered any combative response. He held Stan's moist hands in his. "Stan, I have to get out. Anything less would destroy any respect I have for myself. I'll explain it to you later. Right now, the Judge is waiting. You'll be all right. The Dragon Lady will understand."

Stan fell to his hands and knees and hung onto both of Ben's legs. "Don't do this. Tell the Judge that you've changed your mind."

Ben pushed his grieving friend aside and walked without looking back at the shaken, defeated man covering his face with both hands.

The hearing was brief. Ben asserted all the legal vagaries for the record. The Judge questioned the prosecutor who had no objection. He addressed the defendant.

"Mr. Harvey, you heard Mr. Russo state that he wants to withdraw from your case on the grounds that the attorney-client relationship has degraded to the point that you need a different attorney. If you do not object, I will give you additional time to retain new counsel. What is your position?"

"Your Honor, Mr. Russo has done an excellent job for me, up to now. But I do need a different attorney to go to trial on my behalf, someone who will pay more attention to my thoughts on trial strategy."

Joe never acknowledged Ben's presence. The Judge nodded.

"All right. Mr. Russo is hereby relieved from any further duty in this matter. Mr. Harvey, appear in this courtroom in thirty days with your new attorney. We'll set the trial date then."

Ben's stiff neck loosened up. The elephant standing on his chest went away. He could not contain his smile as he skipped out of the courtroom. He did not notice the tall, thin Asian woman sitting in the back row. Her dark sunglasses hid her eyes, which were memorizing him from head to toe.

Chapter 17

Ben knew what he had to do for his fallen comrade and for the young lady he had come to know. The meeting took place behind closed doors in Delores' office, with only the three of them present.

"Candy, I am out of the case but not out of your life unless you want me to be. Please listen to what I have to say. We do not know if your dad's parents are still alive and would want to see you, have a relationship with you. We do not know anything yet. You are the only child of their son who died defending his country, in your country. I want to try to find them, advise them of your existence, their granddaughter. Only if you want me to. There are no guarantees. You are strong, intelligent, know your own mind. Do you want me to go forward, or leave it alone?"

Candy raised her eyes for the first time. Her legs shook as she sat on the couch. "All my life, I felt like I was torn apart, cut in pieces, not whole. Other people know who they are, where they come from, who made them. My mother did not want to talk about it. I forgave her a long time ago. I thought about that many times. Maybe she believed it was best for me not to know that I would say something to the wrong people who would do me harm—make me an outcast, forever, by my own people."

She stood up and walked over to Ben sitting in a chair several feet away. "When you told me that my dad was your friend, a soldier, who loved my mother, I felt alive, free, not a prisoner of my own bad thoughts. I am somebody, not just a bad girl who gives pleasure to strange men for money. My mother loved this man. Love made me, I am so proud of that." She knelt down on her knees before him and looked into his eyes. "But my mother's love was taken away from me. Alone again. If I can't have my father's love either, maybe his parents can…learn to love me. I want that, need that, pray for that."

Her body crumbled in a heap before his feet, her face flushed to the floor, no sound coming from her. Ben gently raised her and put his face close to hers.

She spoke without expression. "Mr. Russo, did you understand what I said?"

Ben tearfully hugged her and whispered. "I understand. I will do my best."

Chapter 18

Ben knew the limits of his investigative skills and his ignorance concerning these newfangled computers that all the other attorneys were buying. He was a dinosaur, relying on one secretary, and a computer that barely accomplished the basics of law practice. He dialed his crusty, good old boy, buddy Tim, a former cop who ran his own investigative firm.

"Hello, Tim Phillips."

"Hey, you old dog. Do you always have to be on speakerphone? Are you still screwing your secretary?"

A roar over the phone. The speaker was off.

"Are you freaking crazy? Don't say shit like that. Karen has a jealous husband. Do you want to get me killed?"

Ben's laugh was loud. "Calm down, you old stud. I need you to find me an older couple, in their seventies. Used to live on Long Island. Owned a Buick dealership. Maybe they're still there or moved to Florida like all the other New York Jews and Italians. Can you help me?"

A sarcastic laugh, almost a grunt, emanated from the other side of the phone. "I'm not a magician. What other information can you give me for starters?"

"Name is Bernie or Bernard Berkman. The dealership was called Berkman's Buick, somewhere near Jones Beach. I don't know if the business is still running or if Mr. Berkman still has anything to do with it. Can you do it? For a reasonable fee?"

Another roar. "You cheap dick! This will cost you. I'll need at least one other guy in New York to help. Maybe other states. You are lucky. I just upgraded my computer system. The big boys were trying to take away all my regular clients."

"Fax me your contract. I'll pay the retainer. This is high priority for me. I need an answer in a few weeks, at the latest."

"Listen, tightwad, you'll get the contract today. I'm surprised you have a fax machine, you cheap fuck."

Ben laughed. "I had to. The other lawyers demanded instant responses after their phone calls. Shit, it's getting harder to make a living out here."

"Tell me about it. Make sure your check clears the bank."

"OK, asshole, enough with the jokes. Talk to you later."

Chapter 19

Ben dreaded anytime his wife, Jennifer, said the magic words, "We have to talk." He preferred his urologist's finger up his anal canal searching for a brittle prostate gland. Now he had to walk the treacherous path of communication with his better half. She was relaxing on the couch reading a book. The girls, Amy and Emma, were in their rooms. He spoke slowly and cautiously.

"I gave up a case that paid good money, but I had no choice. My client has given me mixed signals about my withdrawal. But he didn't make a big deal of it the last time I saw him."

She put the book down and looked at him. "You never tell me about your cases. Why are you doing this now? Mixed signals? What does that mean?"

Ben went to the refrigerator and got a beer. He needed help on this one. "Do you want anything from the refrigerator?"

She shook her head. "What's going on, Ben? Do you owe someone money?"

He took a healthy swig. "Nothing about money. Maybe I'm overreacting. But I thought you should know."

She got up and folded her arms. He knew the look. The words stammered out.

"This guy, a strange guy, charged with sexually exploiting minor girls—a referral from Stan Klein—huge retainer. Maybe I shouldn't have taken it, but the money…"

She screamed. "Sexually exploiting girls? What kinds of cases are you taking? Give this person his money back! Now!"

"I gave it back. He doesn't care about that."

"So, what does he want? Whatever it is, do it!"

He reached for some inner strength. He had to tell her. "One day, in my office, he threatened the family, me, you—even the girls—saying that they'd be in danger if I abandoned him as a client."

Her voice reached a higher octave. "Danger? What kind of danger? Did you tell the police?"

"He said that girls that age can be taken away, kidnapped, to places far away—to be trained to be prostitutes."

She looked toward the girls' bedrooms, listened, wanted to make sure they were in their rooms. Her face was on his. "You kept this to yourself? You put our kids in danger? Tell the cops—the prosecutor."

He sat down on the couch, put his beer on the floor, and his hands over his face. "Jennifer, he's smart. He'll deny it. His word against mine. In court, he accepted my withdrawal without showing any objection or anger toward me. Even if they believed me, all the cops would do is warn him not to make any more threats."

Ben got up, walked over to her, peered into her scary eyes. "I almost did not tell you. Nothing I can do now. But you needed to know."

He hung his head low. She hesitated, thought to herself, grabbed his face, and quietly said. "No one, and I mean no one, is going to hurt our girls. We are going to be very careful from now on—totally chaperoned. We're taking our guns out of storage, back in the house again, locked and loaded…until this pervert gets convicted and goes away for a long time."

Her speech reminded him why he fell in love with her and married her. His bluster as a lawyer was just a camouflage, a mirage, to hide his weakness and insecurity. She was strong, resilient, tough. He needed her to enable him to survive his crazy roller-coaster life. He meekly asked, "Should we tell the girls?"

She held on to his cheeks. "Hell no. When is this former client going to trial?"

"Within a few months."

"Good. I hope that he rots in prison for the rest of his life."

There were limits to Ben's courage. He dare not tell her what Stan Klein said about the Dragon Lady. That evening, he prayed, a rare occurrence for him. He asked God for help, strength, and the protection of his wife and children. He felt unworthy to ask God for his own well-being since he had disappointed Him so many times.

Chapter 20

Ben always started the day reading the paper, first obsessing on the sports section and then the obituaries. He enjoyed looking at the photos of the decedents, especially those taken decades before death arrived and then at the end stage of life. How beautiful and handsome everyone used to be. How could the person in the second photo be the same person in the first? He wondered how anyone could recognize a classmate at a 50th reunion.

His hand shook and almost tipped over his full cup of coffee when he noticed the photo. A short obituary followed.

> "Stanley David Klein, 69 years old, renowned criminal attorney for over 40 years, passed away on April 11, 1986. A memorial service on his behalf will be held on Friday, April 14, at Temple Emanuel at 10 am. Rabbi Levi Cohen will preside. The family requests that any donations be made to the American Heart Association."

He mumbled to himself and thought.

"Stan is dead? A heart problem? Wow, Jews do not waste time in burying the dead. Divorced—two sons in Phoenix. Never met them—supposed to be successful businessmen. I hope I get to talk to them tomorrow."

Many came to show their respects for Stan, an old-time lawyer—never give up—fight to the end. But to his close-knit group of colleagues and friends, he was a charmer, cordial, and interested in your welfare.

Ben first saw Margarita, Stan's primary legal assistant, and paralegal. Her love and admiration for her boss was obvious to anyone who ever visited his office. A plump fifty-year-old married woman, there were rumors that they were lovers decades earlier. One of the many reasons Stan's wife divorced him. In his earlier life, he successfully bedded many young, beautiful women. She was standing alone wearing a black dress. Her eyes were bulbous and red. She held a handkerchief in her hand, and mascara was running down her cheek. He hugged her. Her perfume was pungent.

"I'm so sorry for your loss. You were with Stan for so many years. I will miss him. Are you OK? How are you doing?"

She cried in her handkerchief and could not speak until her sobs subsided. She softly spoke.

"Oh, I loved that man, such a gentleman—so kind to me. I've been with him for over twenty-five years. Taught me everything I know. I don't know what I'm going to do now."

Ben hesitated, then asked, "What happened? Did he pass out in the office?"

"Oh, no. The other day, I'm getting my days all mixed up. He never came in. I called his home. No answer. After a few hours, I got so worried. Drove over there. Knocked on the door; it was unlocked. I saw him lying on the floor of the kitchen. He was not breathing. I called 911. The paramedics thought it was a heart attack."

Her sobs erupted again. Ben knew that he could not push too hard, but he had to ask.

"Margarita, just one question. Did Stan ever mention a client of his—an Asian woman? Possibly with the nickname 'Dragon Lady?'"

She looked away when she answered, "No, no, nothing like that." She walked toward the entrance to the temple and never looked back.

Mostly lawyers and their staffs comprised the one hundred or so who attended. Several speakers emoted about Stan's kindness, charitable nature, love of the law, and most importantly how great a father and grandfather he was. Even a few prosecutors teared up during the eulogies. Peter and Matthew Klein sat with their families and stared at the red carpet throughout the entire service.

Ben made sure that he was at the very end of the line of people giving their condolences to the grieving sons. He asked for a moment to speak to them. The oldest son, Peter, grimaced when he said, "There are so many things we still need to do today. The ashes, the urn, the burial."

Ben persisted. "Was an autopsy done by the Medical Examiner to determine the cause of death? I did know that your dad had heart problems."

Peter's face turned beet red. "What are you trying to say? He was an old man who died of a heart attack. He's been cremated. His wishes. Do you see that urn over there? Just because he represented drug dealers doesn't mean that drugs had anything to do with his death. Don't start any rumors! Get out of my way and fuck off!"

Matthew shook his head and turned to Ben. "I'm sorry my brother talked to you that way. He's now the head of the family, has to make some major decisions—under a lot of pressure. My dad did not do drugs. He was taking blood thinners because of very high cholesterol. Anyway, thanks for coming to Dad's service. Nice meeting you."

Ben's chin was on his shoulder as he walked to his car. He thought. "Why the hell did I bother these people? With all the grief they are going through. Sometimes I can be such an asshole."

He did not notice the tall, slim Asian lady staring at him through her dark glasses from the back of the four-door Lexus sedan parked behind his red Granada. He drove away. She told her driver to take the long way back to her hotel. She wanted to see the canyons filled with rabbits, birds, coyotes, javelinas, bobcats, lizards, snakes, and assorted other creatures. She loved all animals. It was just human beings she had a problem with.

Chapter 21

Ben's secretary buzzed and startled him out of one of his daydreams. "Tim, the investigator is on the phone."

Before he could say anything, Tim yelled out. No speakerphone was on. "Now is that the woman you are banging? She sounds nice. What does she look like? Does she wear short skirts? Does she…"

"Shut up, you asshole. She could probably hear your loudmouth. Her husband would stick a pole up my rear if he believed that!"

"Well, tightwad, you've probably had a lot of objects up there already. You did go to law school in San Francisco, didn't you?"

He laughed until he had to catch his breath. "Anyway, I've found your man, his wife too. The Berkmans are in their seventies, retired, live in Sarasota, Florida. All alone. Their other son and three grandchildren all live on Long Island. They only see them during the Christmas holidays and for part of the summer."

Ben asked, "Did you have a long conversation with them? Tell them anything about me?"

"Nothing to tell. You never told me anything. I did tell them that Arizona attorney, Ben, needed to talk to them about something important. They were very friendly. Nice people.

"I'm faxing the contact information to your office, along with my final bill. Are you going to pay me? I had to hire a Tampa investigator. Should I wait to get paid before I send you my report?"

Ben laughed. "I'll pay you right away. You'll get the check tomorrow. I promise. I made some money on a P.I. case a few weeks ago. I'm good, at least for a while. Talk to you later."

Another interruption from the secretary. "Jennifer's on the phone. She sounds pissed."

He sighed. "Yes, dear?"

She yelled. "What the hell is going on? The same two cars near the front of the house two times today. When I opened the shades to look, one car leaves, and the other one shows up a little later. I'm scared—what should we do?"

He spoke very deliberately. "The trial is in about a month. After that, we'll have no problems. Do you remember the models of the cars? The license plate numbers? Would you recognize the drivers?"

"No, each guy wore some type of hat—like what you see in movies made in Japan, China. Maybe a Toyota and a Honda? Are you coming home soon?"

"I'll be home in an hour. Pick up the girls early from school today. From now on, I'll drive them in the morning and pick them up in the afternoon. No more busses or friends taking them. Do you understand?"

Jennifer was quick with her response. "I'm leaving now. We'll talk when you get home."

Ben's stomach acid increased and heartburn took over. Only 3 pm. He mumbled.

"Fuck it." He grabbed his Irish whiskey and poured himself a solid double.

Chapter 22

Ben made the call. He had no road map, script nor blueprint as to how he was going to introduce himself, inform them about his friendship with Scott and then Candy, Mona, and everything in-between. No plan could ever be devised to take the conversation neatly from point A to B to C. It would be "the long and winding road" that Paul McCartney sang about.

When Alice Berkman picked up the phone and sweetly said, "Hello," he quietly cried. It took him a few seconds to respond.

"Mrs. Berkman, my name is Ben Russo, an Arizona attorney. May I call you Alice? Is your husband Bernard also available?"

He heard Mr. Berkman in the background. "Alice, is that the Arizona lawyer? Is it?"

Ben raised his voice. "Sir, Mr. Berkman, Bernard, can you hear me? This is going to be a long phone call. Do you have an extension to listen in on? Both you and Alice need to hear me and to ask any questions you may have."

The next forty-five minutes were sad, happy, joyous, and euphoric. The grieving parents wanted to know more details concerning Scott's death, answers that the military refused to give. As he filled in the spaces, Ben felt the same pain and anguish as he did on the day his best friend passed from this earth. He did not want to spend time being emotional on the phone, but he could not help himself. Through their patience and reassuring words, Bernard and Alice acknowledged that the pauses reflected moments of profound sadness on the other side of the phone.

When the Berkmans heard about Mona and Candy, it was their turn to lose their composure. Ben heard gasps, deep breathing, sighs, coughing, and the blowing of noses. Bernard spoke first. "You said that Scott had a child, a daughter, a Viet Namese girl? Please tell me if I got that right."

"Yes sir, you got it."

Ben heard Alice's tormented voice. "Scott, Scott, I miss you so much. Bernie, a girl—our granddaughter."

They were now together on the same phone. Alice pleaded. "When can we see her? We'll fly there. When?"

Ben paused to gather himself in order to be able to say a few intelligible words.

Bernard yelled, "Ben, are you there? Ben?"

"Yes, Bernard, Alice, I'm here. I will call you back as soon as I have talked to Candy. I…loved your son, I will cherish our conversation today for the rest of my life."

Alice chuckled. "I know you are not Jewish, but I say Shalom to you anyway. You are a good boy. You will never know how happy you made Bernie and me. God bless you."

Ben gently hung up the phone. He felt like he had cotton shoved down his throat and that someone had thrown a bucket of water on him.

Chapter 23

Delores demanded that the meeting between the Berkmans and Candy take place at 5 pm in the main conference room of the County Prosecutor's Office. No one, not even her supervisors, would know of this event. They would tell her that it was too risky. They had Candy in a secret location. This could blow her cover. Why did she need to get personally involved in the drama of this family? She was a prosecutor, not the moderator of *This Is Your Life.* After all, the trial was in two weeks.

Ben, Alice, and Bernard walked the two short blocks from his office to the prosecutor's office in silence. The shared anxiety prevented a word from being spoken. When the elevator door opened, Delores smiled, said hello, and despite her red, puffy eyes and runny nose, was able to say, "Mr. and Mrs. Berkman, this is Candy, your—granddaughter."

Ben concentrated, since he wanted a picture, a mental image of this moment embedded in his psyche forever. Candy, dressed in a fluffy pink blouse and light blue pants, looked more than beautiful. She walked slowly, deliberatively, toward the Berkmans, who were stiff, overwhelmed, bewildered. She softly kissed Alice on the cheek and touched Bernie's shoulder. An avalanche of love erupted. They raised her off the ground and twirled her several times until they were dizzy. No one spoke and no tears until Candy took one hand from each and said, "I love you, Grandma and Grandpa."

Ben was absorbed into a cloud and bubble of goodness and love.

Chapter 24

Delores knew that by 6 pm, they all had to leave. Her secure parking lot would close at 6:30, and she needed to take Candy to her secret location. She hated to interrupt the magic.

"Candy, everyone, we have to go. My parking garage closes in thirty minutes; I have to drive Candy to where she is staying."

Bernie smiled when he asked, "Let's all celebrate, a dinner together, my treat. We are staying at La Paloma. Meet us there in the main dining room. Alice and I have a rental car; we wanted a Buick. All they had was a Cadillac!"

All eyes looked at Delores. Her brain and heart were dueling each other. She paused, finally said, "I am concerned. We have to be careful. Ben, walk with me and Candy to my car. I'll drive you to yours. It is best we use separate cars."

Alice and Bernie hugged and kissed Candy, again told her that they loved her and would take care of her for the rest of their lives. Candy shyly said, "I love you. See you soon."

Chapter 25

The county public parking lot was supposed to be open and secured by two sets of security guards. The rotating shifts started at 6 am and ended at 7 pm. Normally, the guards would do a routine walk of the county area surrounding the lot before closing the doors of the fifty-year-old garage. No one would be able to open these doors after 6:30 pm without two keys that only the commander of the guards possessed. He was long gone until 6 am when he would arrive to allow early bird employees to park their cars and start work. Ben was concerned. He advised Delores that he did not see either parking guard. She was calm.

"They probably started their rounds early. These guys are always trying to steal time from their employer."

Ben nodded and grinned for Candy's sake. "OK, I'll stay at the entrance. Just in case. Pick me up when you exit."

Delores and Candy turned the corner. Almost immediately, Ben felt a stiff object pushing into the back of his skull, right above his right ear.

"Don't say a word, asshole, if you ever want to see your kids again."

He recognized the voice of Joe Harvey. Lola and two Samoans, each the size of a grizzly bear, emerged from behind the bushes. Joe put his finger to his mouth and told them to be quiet. He looked into the garage and saw the sedan slowly approaching. He whispered to the Samoans.

"Take off now. Hurry. Meet me at the house. I have this covered. Will be there soon."

When the vehicle stopped, Joe grabbed Ben by the collar and ran to the driver's side. He pointed the large pistol at the driver's head and then at Ben's head. The window was partially open.

"Delores, get the fuck out. Get in the back. You too, Candy. Don't make me kill all of you."

After Joe and the two ladies were crunched in the back, Candy in the middle, he yelled to Lola. "Take the wheel and drive to the house. No freeway. Just go through the streets, the back way."

Joe jumped into the front passenger seat, turned immediately to the back, and quietly said, "If I hear a sound, anything, from any of you, Candy gets it first."

Delores could not restrain herself. "What do you want with us? Are you crazy? You're making it worse for yourself."

He pointed the gun directly at the prosecutor's head. "Shut the fuck up, bitch. One more word and you and this little snitch will get it together. I have some questions. We'll be there soon. Do anything stupid and your time will end in the back of this car."

His face was drenched with sweat. Lola tried not to show that she was shaking in her cowboy boots. She started the engine and burned rubber in the parking lot. Joe turned and yelled.

"Slow down! Don't speed. Only a few miles away. We don't need any attention from nosy cops."

Ben then felt something, a presence, an essence, energy, as he had experienced in the past. The car suddenly jolted ahead at an outrageous speed, twisted and turned between several oncoming vehicles, and drove through two stop signs.

Lola screamed, turned to Joe, whose glare was scary. "I can't stop it! It's on its own!"

He somehow jumped over her, pushed her out of the way, grabbed the steering wheel, and stomped on the brake pedal over and over. He pulled on the brake handle before he screamed.

"What the fuck is going on?"

His eyes widened when he saw the steps of a building in front of him. He dropped the gun when he put both arms over his face as the sedan crashed through the main door of the Tucson Police Department and stopped. Within seconds, twenty very angry cops surrounded the smoking vehicle with guns pointed at all the occupants.

After the smoke cleared, literally and figuratively, and after interviewing Delores and Ben, they put Joe and Lola in handcuffs. Lola cried and screamed to anyone who would listen and said that Joe kidnapped her and had no idea who he was.

Ben turned down the cops' offer to drive him to his parked vehicle close to a mile away. He needed some fresh air, some time alone to clear his head. He wondered, "What the hell happened back there?" The rainbow sunset was beginning to descend under the horizon. He mumbled to himself. "Getting dark. I'd better hurry up."

Before another step was taken, he stopped in his tracks, grabbed for his glasses, and looked up.

"What is that? Going higher and higher. Looks like bumblebee wings on a man! A bird? Holy shit!" The vision disappeared into the heavens. He scratched his head and quickened his pace and thought. "I must be going crazy."

Chapter 26

The customs agent at the Los Angeles airport took a close look at the tall, Asian lady wearing dark, tinted glasses. "Are those prescription glasses, Ms…uh…Dora Chen?"

"Yes, they are, sir. The sun bothers my eyes."

"Can I see your passport again, please?"

He saw nothing unusual in the Brazilian passport. He smiled. "Really none of my business, but you do not look Brazilian."

She took another object out of her purse, handed it to him, and smiled back. "Dual citizenship with Thailand."

The agent paused, returned both passports to the lady, and cordially waved. "Have a great time in Rio."

One day later, the Dragon Lady in Portuguese thanked the porter for helping with the luggage and gave him a big tip. She double-locked the outside door of her suite at the five-star hotel. When she opened the sliding glass door, she felt the ocean breeze in her face and admired the tenacity and sound of the waves repeatedly crashing into the white sandy beach glowing and sparkling from the rays of the sun. She took her glasses off to get a better look at the seagulls chirping, crying, and soaring above.

Chapter 27

Four years and many Irish whiskeys later, Ben opened up the large envelope mailed from Sarasota, Florida. Several photos of Candy, Alice, and Bernie together, smiling, on the campus of the University of Florida. He resisted the urge to show emotion, knowing that his secretary was right outside the door. He pressed his thumb across their faces and thought.

"God, Candy is so beautiful. Looks a lot like Scott. The same smile. Bernie and Alice look younger than when they were here."

He noticed the short note.

Dear Mr. Russo, Ben:
> I now call myself Mona, after my mom. I am so happy. I just started college. Because of you, I am going to study criminology.
> Maybe I'll become an attorney like you! You are the best. I never told you that I love you and will never forget you. You have made my life so wonderful. If you are ever in Florida, please visit me.

> Your friend forever,
> Mona (Candy)

P.S. My grandma and grandpa also say hello and love you.

This time he could not stop the tears rolling down his cheeks. The sound of the beeping phone brought him back to the present.

"Ben, Steve Stone on the phone again. He is pissed off at us for ignoring him the last few days. His wife locked him out of the house. He wants to know what you can do. Remember, he still owes you money from his last case."

Ben carefully put the letter and photos in his desk drawer. He sighed. "Put him through."

Another day in paradise.

Chapter 28

Ben felt good about himself that day. Twenty-two years in practice, fifty years old, substantial trial experience, modestly financially successful, a loving wife, two daughters in college. He was alone. His secretary had left early for lunch. The tall, thin blonde startled him as she came into his office. She did not make eye contact when she spoke. "Can you help me? I'm in trouble. My name is Joy Tweet."

Her eyes remained pointed toward the ground. He felt generous and did not sense any alarm bells. "Sure, sit down, Ms. Tweet? Take your time—the whole story."

She stared at him. "I'm bipolar—supposed to be on medication. But not on that day. I was hungry—went into a food store. I had a few dollars. I wanted to buy a loaf of bread, maybe some chocolate milk. It gives me energy, makes me feel better for a while. People stared at me, especially the man stocking the shelves. I got scared."

Her whole body shook. He got up and handed her a cup of water from his dispenser.

"Everything's OK. I'm listening."

"I cried, grabbed some candy bars, and ran out. A man from the store grabbed my arm. Look, I still have bruises. He yelled at me, was mean to me, and called the police. I spent two days in jail. The Judge let me out if I promised to stay in Tucson."

"Your name is Joy?"

"Yes, Mr…"

"Russo, Ben Russo. Do you have a lawyer?"

"I have no lawyer. But the lady in Court told me that all I had to do was sign a piece of paper and never go back to the store. Then they will drop the charge of shoplifting and leave me alone."

"Who gave you my name—how to contact me?"

"The nice lady typing in the courtroom."

"You mean the court reporter?"

No response, just a confused look.

"Show me your paperwork. Judge Arnold, Justice Court. You have to go back to Court next week." He thought hard for a few seconds as he stared at the slumping, cowering figure before him. She appeared to be getting smaller, as if she were morphing into a fetal position. He sighed. "So, you want me to help you?"

Her glassy, moist eyes got larger. "Please, please. I don't want to go back to jail. The other girls called me names, hit me, took away my food."

Ben stood up, walked to the window, admired the blue/green mountains, and softly said, "You don't have any money, do you? I mean for my services."

She studied the thick, turquoise carpet and held her hands tightly together. "I can...I will do things for you."

She approached him, stared at his crotch area, and slowly lifted her long, soiled dress higher and higher, past her knees, then mid-thigh, and then—

He yelled. "Stop that. Sit down!"

She persisted. "I can do other things, you know." Her mouth opened wide. She was now within a few feet from him. He stumbled backward and hit his head on the glass-enclosed map of Sicily hanging on his back wall.

"No, no, go back—now!"

She flopped back into the soft leather chair and cried through her hands.

"Listen, I'll help you. No charge. But you'll sign the paper and not go back to the store, right?"

A high-pitched squeaky voice emanated from the twisted, seated form. "Yes, yes, help me. I don't want those girls to hurt me anymore."

"OK, come back next Wednesday, the 10th of the month. I'll go to Court with you. Make sure you are here. Remember, do not do anything—bad. I'll keep the Court paper."

"I'll be good. I'll be good."

He called to her as she got up to walk toward the door. "Joy, do you have a doctor? Are you on any medication?"

"I'm on AHCCCS, El Rio Center."

She fumbled in her large brown grocery bag. "Here are my pills."

He recognized the doctor's name on the script. He had met her many years ago when he accepted court appointments. The drugs were widely prescribed for bipolar disorder, depression, and anxiety.

"I take each of them in the morning and at night. The red one helps me sleep."

"OK, Joy, please stay out of trouble and danger. Do you have a place to stay? You're not living on the street?"

Her eyes descended. "Well, I know an older man who lets me stay with him as long as I cook for him and do other things. I don't know the address."

Ben cringed, and the furrows on his head appeared. "Well, just so I know where you live, bring this man with you next week to the office. Wednesday, 10 am."

Her smile displayed dark brown dentures with a bottom row of teeth crisscrossing one another. "Thank you, sir, Mr. Russo."

He looked at his watch. Almost lunchtime. He needed to check out a few things, just in case, to be safe.

Chapter 29

He knew most of the court reporters, but he didn't know why a J.P. Judge would need one for misdemeanor arraignments that took only five minutes. "I wonder if Sue Miller referred Ms. Tweet to me."

He wandered around a few of the places that court personnel eat lunch in downtown Tucson and quickly ate a sandwich at the sub shop. As he walked toward his office, he spotted several court reporters that he really did not know.

"Hey, ladies, are the J.P.'s using court reporters for arraignments now? Judge Arnold had one a few days ago?"

The women smiled. They've seen him around a long time. One pretty thirty-year-old responded. "We're mostly in Superior Court. I know that Karen Bolding just got assigned to JP Court. I don't think she likes it very much. She's stuck with all the Judges, on whatever they need. She floats around a lot."

Ben could not stop himself. He thought of himself as a stand-up comic. "Yeah, I wish I could float out of Tucson this month. It will be 100 degrees for the next two weeks. Anyway, could you ask Ms. Bolding to call me? Here's my card—if she gets a chance. I'd appreciate it."

Several hours later, as he was about to turn off the lights at his office, the phone rang. "Shit, almost six o'clock; who's going to bother me now?"

He heard a female voice. "Hello, this is Karen Bolding. Is Ben, Mr. Russo there?"

"Hey, Karen, it looks like you're working late."

"You got it. I'm stuck for the next few months in JP Court. The Judges decided that they needed a court reporter because of all the bad publicity they've been receiving for not releasing enough defendants for petty crimes. The jail is crowded with dope smokers and minor thieves."

"Well, talking about an alleged thief, did you notice a young lady, very thin, looks like a street person, get released a few days ago by Judge Arnold? I met the woman. She said that a nice lady gave her my name."

"Gee, Ben, I hope that I didn't cause you any problems. Sue Miller told me about you. I felt so sorry for her. She looked so lost, confused, crying, hysterical. The Judge felt the same way. What she stole a few candy bars? But I apologize if she's bothered you in any way."

"No, no, Karen. I appreciate the referral. All lawyers need to step up to the plate and help the most needy. Anyway, I wanted to thank you." He laughed as he said, "But, you know, I also represent rich people. So, don't be shy in giving my name out to those folks also."

"OK, Ben. I'll do that. I better get home now before my husband thinks that I'm in jail now. Good luck."

Ben thought that it was nice that Sue Miller thought that he was a good lawyer. He'd have to take her out to lunch. His wife would not get jealous. After all, Sue was sixty-five years old and hit the scales at about 250 pounds. It would be a long, expensive lunch. He liked talking to her. She spit out her food as much as he did as she ate. They needed shower curtains for protection from the debris of food particles spiriting out of their mouths.

Chapter 30

Ben was glad that Joy brought in her friend, a man probably in his early fifties. She was so much cleaner this time. Her hair was shiny; her clothes pressed; and she wore real shoes. The sandals she previously wore had exposed her dusty feet and unkempt toenails.

"Mr. Russo, this is my friend, Carl. He is also my landlord."

Ben stuck out his hand to the balding man with several days' growth of facial hair. As they shook hands, he felt the other's strength and thick callouses. Each avoided eye contact and looked over the other man's shoulder.

"Nice to meet you, Carl. I'm happy that you're providing a place for Joy to stay. Please sit down."

Carl made a half-smile and leaned back in the chair. He wore shiny cowboy boots, old worn-out jeans, and a faded cowboy shirt.

Ben grinned. "It looks like you take good care of those boots, Carl. Did you shine them up or did Joy?"

He was surprised, in disbelief.

"Hell, no! That's why I didn't mind coming down here. Nobody shines boots like the old Mexican across the street from the courthouse."

Joy softly asked, "Is everything going to go all right in court today? I'm not going back to jail, am I?" Her hands touched her face. Carl stared at her with pity and disdain.

"No, no, I'm filing papers today on your behalf. Then you'll sign the agreement they offered. I have been told that most of the stores are allowing first-time offenders to avoid a conviction."

Carl blurted out. "A first-time offender? Are you kidding me?"

His brownish/green teeth showed through his smirk. Joy wished that there was a hole she could crawl into.

Ben calmly spoke, "Listen, I don't know Joy very well, but she's been through a lot. What the prosecutor is unaware of is not my concern. Let's go."

When they entered, Karen Bolding smiled at Ben. The Judge and the prosecutor treated Joy with respect and dignity, and the case was dismissed. The Judge grinned and gently counseled her. "Ms. Tweet, I know that I will never see you again under these circumstances. I wish you the absolute best."

Carl mumbled as he walked out of the courtroom. "What a fucking joke!"

Joy grabbed Ben's hand. "Thank you so much, Mr. Russo. God bless you. Carl is really a good person, but some days…"

"Don't worry about that. Take good care of yourself, and listen to your doctor. Call me if you need me—for anything. By the way, do you have family in Arizona?"

"My mother lives in Casa Grande. Haven't seen her for almost a year. I should go visit her."

"That's right. Family is most important. Just in case I need to contact you, you did put your current address on the court papers?"

"Yes, that's where I will be staying."

"All right, good luck to you in all ways."

She ran to catch up to Carl, who by now was visibly agitated in his pickup truck.

Chapter 31

Ben felt complacent that Friday morning. Not much to do that day, other than a bar luncheon that he looked forward to. He loved to say things quietly at his table of friends that the speakers and other elitists could not hear. He would mumble: "What a bunch of windbags, pontificating as usual. Most of these tight asses have never seen the inside of a courtroom, and they are giving us advice?"

He studied the photos of his daughters, now nineteen and twenty-one, both in college. He was so proud. One a sophomore at UCLA, and the other a junior at Berkeley. They both loved California. He knew that it was his fault. He took them to the beaches and up the coast too many times on vacations. They'd probably stay in California after they graduated. He groaned, felt empty inside. His secretary walked in and handed him the paper. Her hands shook.

"Have you read this article? Isn't that the lady you represented several months ago?"

"I just glanced at the paper this morning. Let me see."

The article read:

> The Pinal County Sheriff's Office has today announced that the body of a twenty-eight-year-old woman was found east of Interstate 10 south of Casa Grande last Friday. Because of some evidence left at the scene and subsequent identification by a family member, the woman has been identified as Joy Tweet. The Sheriff indicated that the decedent suffered multiple blunt force injuries that appeared to be the cause of death. No other information is available. An autopsy will be conducted by the Pinal County Coroner's Office.

Ben's stomach churned and unhealthy noises emanated from his insides. His head throbbed above both jaw joints. He screamed. "What the fuck is wrong with this world? Oh, my God—I should have done more for this woman. I discarded her because she was poor and had some mental issues."

"Ben, you helped her and did not even charge her. How could you have known that something like this would happen to her?"

He felt the urge to grab his bottle and chug some whiskey, but it was only 10 am, and he would feel embarrassed in front of his secretary.

"Lynn, I have to find out if Joy ever visited her mother in Casa Grande. I assume her last name is Tweet. Try to find a phone number and an address of her. Also, call my crew of buddies and advise them that I won't be at the luncheon today. Just tell them that something came up."

He left the room and walked into the bathroom. He had not thrown up for a long time. The dry heaves and gagging persisted for twenty minutes. When he exited the stall, his face and shirt were drenched with sweat. He gathered himself to make a phone call to a prosecutor friend in Florence.

Chapter 32

Ben was advised that Joy Tweet had been beaten to death with something made of wood. Her bloodied, naked body, underwear, and wood splinters were found one hundred feet east of the freeway in a gully. Ladies' flip-flops were located deeper into the desert. The investigators also noted worn tire tracks, probably from a truck or SUV, adjacent to the line dividing the desert from the freeway.

Ben had to decide what to do first. Lynn had found the phone number and address of a Ruth Tweet. The Florence prosecutor told him that Ruth had identified the body but had not seen her daughter for over a year. Evidently, some recent phone calls between the mother and daughter had taken place. He told Ben that there was no reason why he could not make a courtesy call to the mother of a former client. When Ben mentioned Carl to the prosecutor, he advised Ben that the gentleman had already been interviewed, supposedly knew nothing, and had no real helpful information. His story was that Joy told him that she was going to hitchhike to Casa Grande to visit her mother. When he was asked by the investigator why he did not give a ride to his friend, he just shrugged his shoulders. When Ben heard this, he knew what he had to do now.

Chapter 33

Ben hated the trip to Casa Grande, especially in the summer. If you broke down, you prayed to God that the highway patrol was nearby. Even if you were skilled in changing tires, which he was not, the effort would likely cause you to faint or at least feel that you were going to faint. It was 5 pm. There would be light until 9 pm. He hoped that the directions Ruth gave him were accurate. She seemed nice on the phone and interested in talking about her only child. Ben surmised that the sounds he heard on the phone were suppressed sobs.

Ben slowed down as he passed the area where the body was found. Other than a few scattered saguaros, the desert had very little foliage. He noticed that the ground sloped downward making it difficult for drivers to see much of anything more than fifty feet east of the freeway. He knew that the State cops patrolled the area at least every hour looking for deserted or overheated cars and people in distress. Because of several lawsuits in the past, the police diligently and regularly drove up and down both sides of the parched highway. Ben wondered, "How did the perpetrator kill Joy, drag her dead body into the desert, return to the vehicle, and not be seen by a passing motorist? Could one person do that? Would he need help? Why were her shoes not next to her body? Was she left dead or was she still alive suffering on the fiery hot desert floor? How long had she been there before being discovered?"

Ben hated going to trailer parks. Every trailer looked the same to him. The owners usually let their dogs run wild. He actually had got bitten a few times before, luckily from small dogs. He had seen many killer dogs gnarling their teeth and attacking the chain-link fence as he walked by. He was vigilant as he opened his car door, looked at the sign that said 320 Oak Lane, and slowly opened the metal front gate. He held tightly onto the swinging door as he listened for the sound of any movement. Suddenly a huge cat ran toward him, causing him to jump back. The older lady smiled and then yelled.

"Patsy, leave our guest alone!"

Ben smiled nervously and asked. "Do you have a dog? I've been bitten by dogs that the owners said never bit anyone else."

It was 5:30 pm and 100 degrees in a remote trailer park. He had little appetite to be polite or politically correct.

"Mr. Russo, Ben, come on in. Nothing to worry about. I had a dog up to a year ago, but old Andy died on me. I really loved him."

Ben approached closer, saw that her eyes had teared up. She was not as old as he originally thought. Probably only a few years older than himself. Her skin was as dry as the desert. The lines in her face were deep and dark. But her light blue glossy eyes twinkled. He reached out, shook her hand, and smiled.

"You have beautiful eyes, just like your daughter Joy."

She looked upward.

"Well, her deceased father, even though he was an asshole, also had blue eyes. That was the only good part of him. He died five years ago, only fifty years old, an alcoholic and a no-good S.O.B. But let's talk about Joy. I have cold pop in the fridge. Do you want a can?"

He at first hesitated, just to be polite, but his throat felt like sandpaper. He also had a sudden urge to pee. "Oh, Mrs. Tweet, Ruth, that would be great. Can I use your bathroom for a second?"

She laughed. "You look like you'll need more than a second. It's ten feet to your left, right past the stove."

He urinated like a racehorse, almost missed the commode a few times. A fly kept revolving around his face as he tried to concentrate. He splashed water on his sweaty face and looked in the mirror. His face was red; his tie was crooked; and the beltline on his pants was closer to his knees than to his belly button. He mumbled. "Fuck, I look like shit."

The smiling lady in the baggy shorts and blouse with all the colors of the rainbow handed him the generic can of diet root beer. He was hoping for a pale ale, maybe even a Bud.

"Do you like diet root beer? It's my favorite flavor. Would you rather have iced water? Sit on the couch."

"No, no, this is great. Thank you."

As he sat deeper into a couch than he had ever before, his wallet slipped out of his pants and fell onto the dusty carpet. He bent down, smelled the odor of cat urine, and gagged. He steadied himself, carefully rose up from the floor, and gingerly sat down. He tightly held the wallet in his left hand. He had a yellow legal pad in the right.

"Ruth, you don't mind if I take notes as we speak? When you get to my age, you forget things."

She sat at the other end of the couch and perkily said, "Why, you young whippersnapper. You're a lot younger than me!"

He snapped back. "Oh, no, come on Ruth, you are well preserved, been in a pickle jar your whole life!"

Her smile showed some serious defects in her dentures. She put a hand through her hair and used a bobby pin to keep her bangs out of her eyes. She winked at him.

"OK, smooth dog, should we talk about Joy, the reason you are here?"

For the next hour, Ben did not interrupt her. Every time she uttered the word 'Joy,' she looked up, toward heaven.

"That poor little girl had a rough life. I should have done more for her, protected her, been a better mother to her."

Ben knew that she spoke the truth, from the heart, unfiltered. Joy Sandy Tweet was born in Oklahoma, the only child of Ruth and Jim Tweet. They soon learned that she was different. Although physically healthy, with no major childhood illnesses, she did not respond to certain cues, wanted to be alone, and did not interact well with other children. Ruth and Jim loved her, did their best, and tried to nurture a normal family setting. Eventually, the normalcy turned to dysfunction.

She could barely speak through the sobbing and tears. "I tried. We tried. But it was really hard. The other kids hated her. The teachers sent her home almost every day. They said that she needed to be placed in a facility for mentally ill children. So that's what we did. When she was eight years old, we brought her to a special home in Tulsa, two hours from the small town where we lived. Jim and I visited her every other weekend. I cleaned a few teachers' houses, and he was the custodian of the local high school. We thought many times of moving to Tulsa to be closer to her, but we had no money. At least we had jobs and a roof over our heads." She stood up and looked at the small window. "We just gave up. Could have done more. We abandoned her to strangers who hurt her, destroyed our child's soul. But he and I did not know." Her groans startled Ben. He stood up and touched her shoulder. The cat strolled over his feet, purred, and closed its eyes.

"Ruth, Mrs. Tweet, none of this is your fault. Do you want a glass of water?" Her eyes were so sad, lifeless, so lacking in hope.

"I'll be okay. Let me take a break."

The rest of the history of Joy Sandy Tweet was not any happier. At the age of sixteen, she left the home at her insistence since the law could not legally keep her. Her return to Jim and Ruth at first was loving, healthy, and whole. But the demons resurfaced, and the cockroaches escaped out of the woodwork. Joy hooked up with the townie kids who ditched school, drank, did heavy drugs, burglarized, and participated in rampant, unprotected sex. When she got pregnant, Jim and Ruth had enough and threw her out of the house. For a period of three years, no communication other than infrequent collect calls occurred. Joy then returned, thin, no longer pregnant, and with no child.

Ben asked. "What happened to the baby?"

"We asked. But she refused to talk about it. We let it be since she started to act normal with us again. That did not last long. Jim and I worked, supported her. Any job she started did not work out. The stress, anger, and frustration got to him. He started drinking again and was verbally abusive to both of us. He gave me an ultimatum, 'Either her or me.' She was twenty-one. Then they had a fight. I got scared and called the police. I was afraid that he was going to hurt her. He was drunk and had a tire iron in his hand. The officers recommended that to keep the peace, she had to leave. I gave her all the cash I had. I cried when she left with her little bag in her hand. The police gave her a ride to the local bus stop." She stood up and touched his hand.

"Ben, you know the rest of the story until her death. She kept in touch by phone on occasion and visited us every year or so. We never asked her what she was doing, and she never volunteered any information. She looked OK, was stable as far as I could see." She walked to the sink and drank a glass of warm water.

"Jim drank and smoked too much. Stubborn. Never listened to me. The doctors warned him that all of his arteries were clogged. The heart attack killed him quick. I found him in the backyard on the ground on his back. He was fixing a tire." She turned to him. "Do you want another pop? Cold water? I wish that I had prepared some food for you."

He stood up. "No, no, I have to leave. You told me on the phone that you moved to Casa Grande three years ago?"

"Right. There was nothing for me in Oklahoma. I had a few friends here. They helped me get a decent job as a bookkeeper. I was always good with numbers."

"Tell me about the last year before she died. Did you talk to her much? Know how she lived?"

"She called me every few weeks, collect. I knew that an older guy let her stay with him. I never spoke with him. All she said was that she missed me and would visit me if she got a ride or had money for the bus. But the last few phone calls were different."

Ben's eyes widened. "In what way, were they different?"

Ruth made a half-smile. "It's not what she said, but how she said it. I know my daughter. Something was bothering her. She said that she really needed to see me."

He started to walk toward the door.

"Don't go yet. The last phone call, a week before she died, she said that Carl's son and his friend came by to visit Carl at his trailer. I asked her about them. She wanted to talk about that when we were alone together in Casa Grande."

He asked, "Did she sound scared?"

"I know that she was scared." She sat down on the couch, petted the purring cat, and put her hands on her thighs. "Why, I do not know."

"Ruth, you have been more than kind talking to me. Again, I am so sorry for your loss. I know that you loved her and that she really loved you and needed you."

As he opened the door to leave, she asked, "Did the police tell you where they found her? Was she already dead?"

He hesitated in order to gather his thoughts. "They told me that Joy was still alive when she was left in the desert." The words just escaped from his mouth.

"But, Ruth, the cops sometimes give opinions without a lot of evidence. Only the Medical Examiner can really tell us what happened." He looked away.

She walked over and grabbed his wrist. "Please tell me, tell me—what you know."

"Ruth, Joy crawled thirty yards toward the freeway, up an embankment, from the gully where she was placed. There was a long blood trail. That's how the patrol officer was able to see her from the road. She was brave, fought to the end, wanted to be found, and not die in the desert all alone. She was on her way to see her mother."

Ben hugged her. Her tears soaked his shoulder. He tried to suppress his emotions, but he failed. The sounds emanating from his nostrils gave him away. They remained entwined until the cat woke up and tried to climb up their legs.

Chapter 34

The puzzle, at least in Ben's mind, was beginning to come together. But he needed more. Why did the cops at first assume that Joy had been raped before she died? Because she had no clothes on? How long had she been on the ground before she died? How much time elapsed before she was found? What were the time, date, and cause of death? Without that, nothing could ever be proved in a courtroom. What would the Medical Examiner say in the autopsy report? It was three weeks since her body was found. Why was the report taking so long? Ruth could help him get a copy. He called her. He couldn't concentrate on any of his other cases.

"Ruth, hi, Ben Russo. You remember we talked about the autopsy report? Are you still on the phone?" He heard some gurgling, throaty sounds. "Are you OK?"

"Ben, Ben, I received the report yesterday in the mail. I don't understand it. The doctor said there were a lot of drugs in her system. Also, puncture wounds on one of her arms. There were bruises. It's complicated. He's not sure of the cause of death."

He again heard the sobs flowing from the other side of the phone.

"Ruth, Ruth, I'll come up there, tomorrow. I'll explain the report to you. See you at noon."

He hung up the phone, made another call to his friend Peter, an assistant Pinal County prosecutor, who always had his nose to the ground and got involved in other prosecutors' cases. He was bored with the mundane burglaries and robberies on his desk. Peter wanted murders, rapes, blood, anything to get his juices flowing. He was relentless.

"Peter, Ben Russo. Do you have a minute?"

For the next forty-five minutes, Peter outlined the crime scene. Ben carefully listened.

"I already told you that Joy crawled thirty yards in the desert before she died. Her body's orifices were completely covered with maggots. To make matters worse, she faced upward. The maggots invaded her eyes, nose, and mouth after she passed. Her skull was fractured in the back. Her body had traces of alcohol, roofies, and a massive amount of heroin. One puncture wound on her arm was relatively fresh. Two others were older based upon the scar tissue. What complicated the crime scene was that a heavy rain soaked the body. Coyotes and hawks competed with the maggots over the decaying flesh."

"Peter, any semen found?"

"None, anywhere."

"My friend, you have an incredible memory. How do you know all of this?"

"You've known me for a long time. I commiserated with the assigned prosecutor who was overwhelmed, frustrated, by all these findings. A lot of information, but not very helpful in finding out who the bad guys are. One thing I left out was that there were a few wood chips in the lady's head. Hell, the Medical Examiner, one of the best in the State, is confused."

"Would the prosecutor talk to me? I'll get permission from Ruth, the decedent's mother. I'll become—what do you call it—the victim's attorney representative."

"No problem. You've done me favors before. I'll call Stan Belman. That's the guy you need to talk to. I'll advise him that you're representing the family. By the way, if he tells you things I haven't mentioned, could you clue me in on it too?"

Ben laughed. "*No problema, Senor. Hasta la proxima.*"

Chapter 35

The cat looked sad and forlorn lying in the corner of the trailer. It took several minutes of counseling before Ruth was able to talk.

"Ben, what does this all mean? Inconclusive as to the cause of death? Does not say what day she died—drugs, puncture wounds in her arm. A fractured skull? Wood chips in her hair? What animal did this to my child?"

"Ruth, I need your permission to be your attorney. Let me explain. The law is that you are also a victim because your daughter died."

"But why do I need an attorney? I have no money to pay you."

"I want no money. Only the right, the privilege, to help you find the monster who killed Joy. Being your attorney allows me to get information in the case that the prosecutor ordinarily would not give out. Do you understand? Do you trust me?"

She blew her nose in her handkerchief. "Oh, absolutely. Why are you doing this? You do not know me."

He maintained his composure wanting to show strength. "I'm doing this for Joy, you—and for all the other girls murdered by the evil surrounding us." He stared deeply into her tearful eyes. "I have a wife and two daughters. I knew Joy. I couldn't live with myself if I didn't try to help."

"God bless you, Ben. Find out everything—and I mean everything, you can. But promise me one thing. You'll tell me the good, the bad, and the ugly. Do you know what I mean?"

"Yes, Ruth, I really enjoyed that movie."

The cat raised its head and stared at them.

Chapter 36

Stan Belman's office was surprisingly small considering that he was the head trial attorney of the office. He did have two windows looking into the parking lot. Boxes of documents, letters, and photos flowed over his desk and slowly descended onto the floor already filled with a scattering of trees of paper. Ben thought he was looking at the edge of a glacier as segments of ice fell into the water. He stared at Ben for a few seconds.

"Look, I'm a prosecutor. You're a defense attorney. Why are you taking up my time? I let you in only in deference to Peter who seems to like you. A few other prosecutors in this office told me that you could be a little, let's say, disingenuous, at times."

Ben knew that he had to be tough and show this bloated windbag that he meant business.

"Mr. Belman, Stan, you have to talk to me. I'm the victim's attorney. Ruth Tweet sent me here. She wants me to find out everything about her daughter's death. You know that I am entitled by the rules to review all the investigative reports in this case. That includes all the police reports, photos, the autopsy report, the whole shebang. Just to be totally candid with you, Ruth shared her copy of the autopsy report with me."

Stan held his ground. "You know, Ben, I mellowed out after I came to Arizona from the Bronx more than thirty years ago for law school. I am not the voracious New Yorker I used to be. You sound like you're from back there. Am I right?"

"Brooklyn."

"Okay, I'll follow the rules, only because I have to. Do not screw up my investigation that's still going on. You see that I didn't say 'fuck'? I am a changed man." He smiled and enjoyed his own joke.

"Listen, we're on the same side. I knew Joy Tweet. I want to help you find the killers, the scum, who murdered her. I'll give you any helpful information I find."

Stan stood up. "I have to be somewhere in five minutes. What makes you so convinced that this is a homicide? Maybe this woman overdosed, and the person she was drugging with panicked and threw her onto the side of the road?"

Ben's eyes reddened. "You know that is horseshit! Did she hit herself in the back of the head and fracture her own skull? Don't fuck with me about this case. I'm not afraid to say 'fuck.' I still have some Brooklyn in me."

"OK, Russo, I'm in a hurry. Anything else?"

"Call the Medical Examiner. Advise him that I will call him to review the autopsy report and the photos. I want complete access to his reports, findings, opinions, you name it. Are you OK with that?"

Stan headed to the door. "Sure, I'll call him. And be respectful to him. He's the best we have. Try not to act like an asshole." He smiled and left Ben alone standing in a pile of papers getting larger and larger.

Chapter 37

The walls of Timothy Reed's office were filled with awards, degrees, professional memberships, and several photos of his blonde wife and three young children. Bachelor of Science at Princeton, a medical degree from Johns Hopkins, graduate training at Stanford and the University of California Hospital in San Francisco. He walked into the tidy, large office. The tall, handsome man stuck out his hand. His face looked like he was about forty but he had the body of a thirty-year-old.

"Ben Russo, is that right? I'm Tim Reed, the Medical Examiner. I have some bottled water. Do you want one?"

"No, no, I'm OK."

"Well, if you change your mind, let me know."

The doctor reached down into the small refrigerator and took a long slug from the bottle. Neither knew who was supposed to speak first. Ben started.

"Dr. Reed, I represent the mother of Joy Tweet, Ruth Tweet, who asked me to find out as much information as I can in reference to the death of her only child. I'm not here to tell you or the prosecutor how to do your jobs. I just need to learn as much as I can, in order to explain to a very distraught woman how her daughter died. I read a copy of the autopsy report. The prosecutor agreed that any photos taken of the victim or the scene of the crime would also be made available to me."

"Ben, you mentioned the word crime, something that I, unfortunately, deal with a lot in my job. This lady's situation leaves me with some doubt as to the cause of death and the time of the death. I have no hesitation telling you that foul play, a crime, occurred. But I am a medical doctor. The phrase 'cause of death' does not neatly fit into this sad situation. As you already know, the back of her skull was fractured by something made of hardwood. There were tiny fragments of wood in the back of her head. Obviously, not self-inflicted. She had some traces of Rohypnol and a massive amount of heroin in her system. One track mark, a needle puncture wound, looked fresh, like within several days. There was scar tissue in two other puncture wounds."

"Do you agree, doctor, that Joy was still alive after she was struck with a wooden object and after being injected with drugs?"

"Absolutely. The crime scene indicated that she crawled thirty yards based upon the tracks of her moving body and some traces of blood. Unfortunately, a heavy rain occurred after she died."

"Your report does not indicate a specific time or even the date of death, is that correct?"

"This examination has frustrated me as much as any I have conducted. I believe that I know what happened, but to say it in a court of law, under oath, troubles me. But I'm going to prepare a supplement to the initial report referencing the stage of development of the maggots found on the decedent's body. She most likely died three days before the police found her. I brainstormed this issue with a former colleague of mine from Stanford. He knows as much about maggots as anyone. You are right. He is a goofy guy. He is fascinated with odd, quirky things. We know that maggots only eat dead tissue. So, if we project backward as to the amount of tissue lost and the speed of consumption, it gives a pretty good idea of when she passed. But the rain, the hawks, and the gnarling coyotes make anything more precise almost impossible to reach. I'm sorry. I've talked too much. I didn't give you a chance to ask questions."

Ben rubbed his forehead. "You mean that convicting the monster or monsters who did this to Joy is not going to happen?"

The doctor stood up. "Ben, you know better than I what happens in a courtroom. There is no physical or trace evidence here. No blood or tissue from anyone else. Listen, not to be too graphic with you, Joy was found lying on her back with all of her orifices open. Once she died, the maggots were laid and penetrated her eyes, nose, even the outside of her vagina. Maggots will eat any dead tissue. Then the rain, dirt, hawks, coyotes…"

"So, what would you need in order to help the prosecutor put this animal in prison?"

"Get me her blood, hair, tissue on clothing, shoes, in a vehicle, on the weapon used. Most of these crazies make mistakes and are very sloppy about cleaning up their messes. Ben, I'm pretty busy today. If anything from this end develops, I'll let you know. You'll do the same for me?"

Ben nodded and smiled. "I do have a question. A medical examiner with your credentials, how did you wind up in Florence, Arizona?"

The doctor smirked. "I was hoping you wouldn't ask. Everybody does. My wife Jane is from New Jersey, went to Rutgers, and became a nurse. I met her in my senior year at Princeton on a blind date. Her parents went into assisted living in Casa Grande. They are in their nineties. She is their only child. She asked me, begged me, to take a job near them. Believe me, I'd rather be in northern California than here. But you know—for better or worse."

Ben stuck out his hand. "Tell me about it."

Chapter 38

Lynn yelled, "Ben, you received a large package of documents in the mail from the Pinal County Attorney's Office. A Stan Belman wrote the cover letter. I made sure that there were no ticking bombs in the box before I opened it up. Only kidding. I know that sometimes you can get aggressive and tick people off!"

"Oh, come on, I've mellowed out. I used to be worse."

Stan Belman was a man of his word. Documents, photos, interviews, reports, diagrams, a plethora of homework for him to review. Almost 5 pm. He could not wait. He took the five pounds of material home with him.

Nothing to Ben was more boring, and a waste of time, than reading the interviews of potential witnesses taken by police officers. So many questions having no relevance to the issues at hand, and the person being questioned usually going on a tangent having nothing to do with what was asked. At least, in this case, Detective Luxford recorded the interview with Carl Anderson, as opposed to taking notes and summarizing them in a report. Before the interview, the detective conducted a cursory surveillance of the residence. A twelve-foot by seventy-foot trailer on an acre lot shared by several other residences. A ten-year-old Ford 150 truck with an eight-foot bed with tires that appeared to be new. A chain-link fence in the back occupied by two barking dogs: a Rottweiler and a German shepherd. A medium-sized shed in the back with a closed lock on it. The detective, without a search warrant, never searched the inside of the truck or asked Carl to open up the shed. When asked who lived in the trailer, the answer was short. "Only me now, since Joy passed away."

Most egregious to Ben, the detective never attempted to interview the neighbors. He thought, "Was it because of the nasty dogs in the yards? The heat of the day? No backup if something went wrong?" He wondered before falling asleep.

"What a worthless, superficial investigation! The cops didn't even try to find the killers."

The dreams were relentless. Over and over again, he saw Joy, nude, dirt infested, and bloody, crawl in the hot desert as the ants and flies invaded her skin. What was she thinking? Did she have any hope left? Her sad, scared eyes woke him up. But what could he do? Why was this his problem? He hardly knew the lady. Some force was pulling him into the abyss, the scary unknown. He felt like his mind had been taken over by parasites eating away, consuming his brain tissue.

Chapter 39

For several days, Ben was abrasive and obnoxious to his wife, secretary, and a few clients. He even gave the mailman a hard time for being late. Lynn's patience ran out. She was fed up. She knew that something was wrong. She had not been teary-eyed at work for a long time.

"Ben, I don't get paid enough to be treated like a worthless idiot. If I'm the cause of this, if something at home is not going right, I am here to help you. Please let me know what I can do."

The visual of the loyal, distraught woman before him broke him out of his self-imposed bubble of despair. He knew what he had to do.

"Lynn, I'm so sorry. It's not you. I'm obsessed with an issue that for now I will keep to myself. Please be patient. I'll snap out of it. I promise." He studied the empathetic face that was seeking answers. "Just understand, there will be times that things, not you, get under my skin, cause me to act like a jerk."

"But no, don't ever think of yourself that way—I…"

"No, no, it's me. Anyway, I need you to find an old file, probably ten years old. Do you remember Jeff Reynolds? I represented him on some criminal charges. Get his file out of storage. Maybe there is some contact information in there. I need to talk to him."

She tried to speak. He stood up.

"Can you do that today, now, as soon as possible?"

Her eyes stared at the carpet before she quietly walked away.

Chapter 40

Jeff Reynolds was a perfect fit for his dilemma. Actually, only forty years old, but looking a lot younger, a petty crook, thief, but not mean. Handsome and smooth. The women really dug his good old boy shtick. When necessary, he'd hang out and use with the low-life druggies and sell a little here and there. He knew all the trailer trash in town. But he was smart, above it all, with a good heart underneath his 'not give a shit' facade. He would not physically hurt anyone. The story went that he returned stolen items when he later found out had belonged to orphans living in a house he burglarized. Jeff never lied to Ben, which he really appreciated, since honesty was so rare with crooks.

Probably off probation and parole by now, Ben called every contact, friend, and neighbor listed in the ten-year-old file. A week later, a phone call.

"Some people tell me that you're looking for me. You don't have to worry about me anymore. I'm still a fuck up, but I don't have to do any of the stupid things I used to do. So, what's up?"

Ben laughed loudly. "So, you're straight now? Why? Did you find God, get religious the last few years?"

"You know, Ben, maybe there is a God. Two years ago, I got lucky. An older lady, about your age, saw through all my bullshit and gave me a chance to stay free. Keep this to yourself, but she's my old parole officer. We hit it off. As soon as my parole terminated, we started living together. She comes from a good family, has a couple of grown children, has money, a good job. No need for me to dive into dumpsters and smelly women anymore."

"Yeah, so what do you do all day while she works and brings home the bacon?"

"I'm the male housewife. Cooking, cleaning, keeping her happy in other ways. You should visit me sometime in the foothills. You still haven't told me why you're snooping around looking for me."

"Jeff, I really need your help. Is there anywhere we can meet where I would feel safe? Not have anyone listen in and find out what favor I am asking of you?"

"Come to the house, Sally's house, on Saturday morning. She'll be there. She's not going to let me do anything that will fuck up my life—our lives. *Capiche*?"

"I didn't know you knew Italian."

"I learned a little in prison from my cellmate. Luckily, he was Italian, not black or Mexican. But all of you are basically the same, aren't you?"

He guffawed at his own joke.

"OK, I'll be there. 10 am. Give me the address, choirboy."

Chapter 41

As he drove northeast of town on that Saturday morning, he viewed the natural fruit of the saguaro cacti on the sprawling, silent desert hills. The red fruit and yellow flowers were blooming. "Wow, this area is beautiful." He drove up the long driveway approaching the triple car garage. He shook his head. "I can't believe that knucklehead lives here—a parole officer? Bullshit. These are the real foothills, not the fake foothills where I live."

He walked to the front door and saw the smiling face of his former client standing next to a tall, silver-haired lady. They were holding hands. He thought, "This has to be a freaking dream. No one's that happy."

"Ben, this is Sally, my one and only."

Jeff looked at her and showed off his remarkably white teeth that only an acid wash could produce. She stuck out her long arm.

"Sally Simpson, Ben. I'm not sure if we ever met before." Her equally white teeth were visible.

"No, I don't think so."

Jeff wore shiny burgundy sandals, white khakis, and a light blue, embroidered, short-sleeved guayabera shirt. She wore equally white khakis and a short-sleeved yellow blouse with light blue trim. Ben guessed that she was in her mid-fifties.

"Now I know who dresses Jeff."

The attached couple simultaneously laughed.

"Yeah, she takes good care of me."

She put her arm around Jeff's shoulder and said, "Ben, let me show you around. We'll sit and talk in the backyard."

A brick, six-foot-high fence surrounded the huge pool. A large patio contained a table with plates filled with cheeses, crackers, strawberries, cookies, and a huge pitcher of iced tea. Two white poodles jumped on Ben's legs and started nipping at his feet. She softly scolded. "Simon, Simone, leave our guest alone."

Jeff immediately lifted them up in his arms and smiled. "I'm sorry. They think they are Pit Bulls protecting us."

She touched Ben's arm. "You're probably wondering how a parole officer could afford this place. Even though it is none of your business, many years ago, I was married to an ophthalmologist, older than me. He dumped me for one of his young nurses. What you see is what I got out of the divorce twenty years ago. He took his practice, the boat, fancy cars. I was satisfied. Beautiful house, no mortgage. I deserved it because of all the abuse I took from him."

Ben softly asked, "Jeff said that you have two children?"

"Yes, both of my sons are doing great. One in LA, one in Seattle. No grandchildren yet, unfortunately. Let's have a snack. Then you can tell me how you need Jeff's special services."

She patiently watched Ben gobbled down his third chocolate chip cookie. His plate was strewn with the crumbs of the crackers and cheeses he consumed. The lining of his glass was coated with debris from the food. His shirt was wet from the tea dribbling down his chin.

"So, are we ready to discuss your proposed plan for Jeff?"

Ben wiped his mouth for the last time with his fourth used napkin.

"Yes, here it is."

For the next fifteen uninterrupted minutes, Ben gave a sincere, impassioned, straightforward speech without a hint of hyperbole. He knew that he could never bullshit Jeff, and he also was under the intense scrutiny of a person trained to decipher fact from fiction. He could not read Sally's mind, but the positive body language of Jeff gave him some hope.

Her eyes showed her seriousness.

"Well, I think this guy, Carl Anderson, is going to see through you two like Swiss cheese. He's going to be suspicious as soon as you go over there. And the neighbors? It's been my experience that these lowlifes stick together. The plan is not going to work."

Jeff was internally conflicted. His legs shook back and forth, the only telltale body language he could not control. She noticed.

"What's the matter, Jeff? Is there something you're not telling us?"

He squirmed, then stood up, studied the pool, and thought. "Do I want to risk everything just so that I can be in the game again? But what about the dead woman? I could also do some good for her mother."

"Yes, I haven't been completely honest with either of you. In my previous life, many years ago, I knew this Carl guy. We did drugs together. He is a real piece of turd, a crook, like I was. The way he treated his wife was gruesome. She left him in the middle of the night and never came back. She was so scared that she abandoned their bratty six-year-old son, Stevie. That kid has got to be in his early twenties by now."

She stared at him. "So what are you saying? You think this Carl guy will trust you because you got high with him fifteen years ago?"

He walked over and took both of her hands in his. "What I am saying, Sally, honey, is that for the past few years, since we became serious, I've been the luckiest man alive. You made my life that way. Maybe the Big Guy above wanted to give me a break, another chance. This poor young lady was brutally murdered. The way Ben tells it, the scumbags who killed her will probably never be punished. Maybe I can help in some way, do the right thing for once in my life. Show the man upstairs that I'm really grateful and have changed my ways."

Silence. Ben knew that he had to slow down the pace and lower the intensity of the situation. He turned to her.

"It looks like you got this guy to be spiritual. He never mentioned 'the Big Guy' to me when I represented him."

She studied the cloudless crystal blue sky, shook her head side to side, and looked at Jeff.

"I am so scared. We are so happy now. But I can tell that you need to do this, to make things right in your mind."

She pivoted toward Ben. "But you—you came to my home and convinced the man I love to possibly chuck it all away because of your desire to be— Sherlock Holmes? I pray for his sake that you know what you're doing."

She walked to the door at the back of the house. Jeff tried to touch her arm. She shooed him away and left. Ben saw the fear in his eyes. He grabbed him by his fancy shirt and placed his eyes close to his.

"We can do this—for Joy—for her mother. It is the right thing to do."

Jeff gave Ben a slight push back to create some distance.

"I'm—with you—but give me a few days. Call me—I need to think."

92

His shoulders slumped as he sauntered toward the gate to the pool. The two dogs followed him. Ben grabbed another large cookie for the road and pranced to his car.

Chapter 42

Three days later. Ben could not wait any longer. He made the call.

"Are you in?"

"I'll do it."

"Let's get together at my office. I've got a few ideas, but I need your input. You and I were always a good team. Tomorrow at 10 am?"

"I'll be there."

Chapter 43

Jeff knew that to get anywhere in Ben's muddled plan, his encounter with Carl had to be perceived as a lucky chance meeting. Carl would see through any bullshit explanation as how he just happened to be in a trailer park of eight mobile homes, each separated by fencing and barbed wire. The owners valued their space and privacy. The junkyard dogs barking and carousing guaranteed that. He was aware of the mentality of these people and the risk involved. On his third attempt, he saw an opportunity. The sign read:

Sam, the handy man-can do almost anything

Trailer No. 6-reasonable rates

Push button on chain-link fence

Jeff looked over the four-foot-high fence and hesitated before pushing the button. No sound. The small yard was unkempt with high weeds that could easily hide any canine predator. The trailer was forty feet away. He was not going to chance it. He kept the door to his pickup open in the event he needed to make a quick getaway. After pushing two more times, he shrugged and mouthed the word "fuck it." As he started the engine, an old small jeep slowly approached and parked behind him. A fortyish lady with dirty blonde hair, wearing jeans, boots, and an embroidered western shirt jumped out.

"You looking for Sam? He should be back soon. Sorry about the button. One of the many things we have to get fixed. I'm Peggy, Sam's girlfriend."

She stuck out her hand, smiled, and showed some missing teeth. He got out of the truck.

"Yeah, I'm Jeff. I was driving around and saw the sign. My old lady has a house that needs some plumbing and tile work done. Does Sam do that? I can pay in cash."

For the next fifteen minutes, his disarming charm and presence descended upon Peggy like waves slapping a beach. He complimented her, laughed at what she said, and treated her with total respect and cordiality. She stroked her uncombed hair and blushed at the attention. When he leaned against the fence, a middle-sized dog came out of nowhere and tried to bite his arm.

"Blackie, go back, go back to the dog house. I'm sorry, Jeff, I thought he was inside with his buddy Jake. It's warm out here. I'm surprised that Sam's not home yet. Do you want to wait inside? I can get you an iced tea, a beer?"

"No, no. I'm sure that Sam and Blackie would not like that. Just have Sam call this number when he gets a chance. It was fun talking to you." He walked toward his truck.

"Are your neighbors as friendly as you are? It looks pretty quiet out here."

Furrows on her forehead appeared. "Well, most of the neighbors are older, keep to themselves. We also keep our distance like most of them. One guy can be surly and nasty at times."

"Oh, yeah, which trailer is that?"

She pointed to one that was furthest away from the park entrance.

"Does he have mean dogs?"

"Are you kidding? Those two crazy animals would tear you a new asshole! Pardon my French."

"Does this fellow—what's his name again?"

"I didn't say—but it's Carl, Carl Anderson."

"Does he live alone?"

"A young woman used to live there with him, but she died about a month ago. She was so nice. So sad. Sometimes his son visits."

Her demeanor changed. "Hey, I've got a few chores to do. I'll tell Sam to call you."

Jeff smiled, waved, and drove away. He thought, "Bingo."

Chapter 44

Ben was conflicted when he talked to Jeff on the phone.

"You know, the more I think about this—I'm worried. Sally's right—too dangerous. Maybe we should forget the whole thing."

"Bullshit! I've been inactive too long. You got my juices flowing again. I want to do it…got to do it."

"What happens if he gets suspicious, smells a rat? You've been out of the trenches for a while. You're probably rusty."

"Fuck the rust. Once you've learned how to ride a bike, it all comes back to you. This guy likes three things. I know what to do to loosen his mouth."

Ben had to ask. "What are the three things?"

"Alcohol, weed, and pussy. He knows my history of success, especially the women part."

Ben frowned and rubbed his forehead. "Please be careful, amigo."

Chapter 45

Sally would tolerate Jeff's occasional excessive drinking but never weed. Her ass would be fired if anyone discovered the stash he kept hidden in the back of the storage shed. He packaged it so carefully that not even the rodents could smell it or get to it. After she left for work, he toked up a little bit in the desert, aired out his shirt, and put it in the hamper. Once in a while, her stare made him wonder if she knew but really did not want to know. He needed to be good, but damn it, life was boring as a kept man. He enjoyed the interaction with the crazies. A few younger Chiquita friends served him well. They smoked dope together, but no sex. Sally would dump him for sure if he did that.

He knew that he had to be lucky and careful. The adrenalin rush took over as he turned on the ignition key. The trailer park on that dusty afternoon was quiet. He slowly circled looking for any chance to engage and allow his charisma and personality to take over. Twice before during the previous week, not even the dogs gave him any attention. He thought:

"Maybe this is never going to work… Fuck…I'll just tell Ben that I tried." When he exited from the dirt road to the asphalt, a large Ford pickup truck passed by. The male driver looked at him. Jeff's temples started to quiver and spasm.

"Was that him? I got to find out."

The man was already out of the truck. Jeff slowly drove by, smiled, and waved his left hand. He put on the brakes, got out, and started his approach.

"Whoa, there. Who are you? I'll unleash my dogs on your sorry ass! Rocky! Bandit!"

Two huge dogs, a Rottweiler and a German shepherd, growled, barked, and lunged, causing the iron gate to vibrate. Jeff stopped in his tracks. His instinct took over.

"Come on, Carl—Jeff Reynolds. I don't look that different, do I?"

The man's mouth slowly produced a smile. "Jesus, is that you? I didn't know you were out of prison. How long has it been?"

"About three years now, you old goat."

Their embrace was real, genuine. They had many good times together before the snitch, an acquaintance of both men, rolled over on Jeff to get less time in prison.

"How did you know I lived here? Anyway, come on in. Let's have a few beers. Stay there for a second. Bandit! Rocky!"

The dogs stared at Jeff as their master locked them into a separate six-foot-high back enclosure in the lot. Within a few minutes, both men inside the air-conditioned large wide mobile home were swallowing Canadian whiskey, washed down by Budweiser.

"What have you been doing since you got out? But first, how did you find me?"

Jeff stood up. "Hey, let me get some weed out of my truck. Then we can talk. You still do weed, don't you?"

Carl smiled. "Whenever I can get some."

After a half bottle of whiskey, a six pack of beer, and a few tokes of weed, Carl believed anything coming out of Jeff's shady mouth.

"So, you see, a coincidence. Peggy mentioned your name. I came out here looking for you, an old friend. But I have to be careful. I have an older lady who takes care of me. In my own way, I take care of her. You know what I mean?"

"Yeah, you were always lucky with the broads."

Jeff took a chance. "Man, this place looks like a guy's cave. No squeeze living here?"

Carl took another shot of the whiskey. "Not for the last month or so. My son Stevie, you remember him, he stays here sometimes. Anyway, we don't need to talk about that. Let's just go down memory lane and get drunker. We had a lot of laughs together."

When all the alcohol and dope had been consumed, Carl was barely awake. Jeff touched the sleepy man's arm. "Yeah, Carl, it was great seeing you again. It's fun to get together with an old friend. I'll call you next week."

Carl could barely wave goodbye. His face was on the kitchen table when Jeff closed the gate behind him. The growling and barking sobered him up a little. When he got home, he threw away his shirt and put on a replacement he always kept in the truck. Sally stared at him when he walked into the kitchen. The dope made him hungry.

"Where have you been? It looks like you had a good time."

He grunted something under his breath, grabbed whatever he could find in the refrigerator, and went outside to the back porch in order to escape the interrogation that was imminent. Within a few minutes, his face, soiled with food particles, was on the table snoring. When he woke up at midnight, he tiptoed into the master bedroom, rolled his body onto the king-sized bed, and placed his moist forehead on the smooth, silk pillow.

Chapter 46

Jeff apprised Ben of the bonding sessions with Carl. Sally was beginning to lose her patience and composure. He was afraid of alienating her, but he was having such a good time drugging and drinking. Even the dogs did not growl at him anymore. He needed another hook to speed things up. Carl volunteered no information on Stevie or his friend, the likely soft spots that would undermine the unyielding, concrete facade that he was facing. He thought of visiting Tina, Joyce, and Suzie, three young, sexy blondes he occasionally toked up with and where he usually got his weed. He arrived at the double-wide sixty-foot-long trailer with the cute pink canopies and knocked. Two cats scratched on the inside screen door.

"Hey, girls, anybody home? It's me, Jeff. I need a favor."

The short, thin blonde with large breasts wearing a skimpy tank top and short shorts opened the door.

"Hi, cutie, come on in. Haven't seen you for a while. Sit down."

He smiled, hugged the young lady, and sat down next to her.

"Tina, do Joyce and Suzie still live with you?"

"Yeah, most of the time. They are both crashed in the back. They went to a fraternity party and got totally smashed. I stayed home. Not interested in those spoiled brats." She grabbed a cigarette, lit it, and slowly blew out smoke from her tight pink lips.

"What kind of favor? Do you need more weed? We're kind of low right now."

He hesitated before speaking. "I hope that I don't regret asking. I need you, three ladies, to be seen by a guy I know. No messing around involved. Just so he gets a peek at you."

She squinted. "This sounds weird. A peek at us? Like naked models? We don't do that."

"No, no. No hanky-panky. Just to drive with me in my truck, say hello to the guy. Then we all leave. You have to look good, like you do now." He smiled.

She put out her cigarette. "You'll have to tell us someday what's really going on. But you've done us a bunch of favors. Anything for you, cutie." She put her hand on his lap and kissed him on the cheek. He very briefly thought about responding, but the sounds of snoring in the background slowed him down. He quickly got up, walked to the door, and carefully stepped over the two cats.

"I'll call you, let you know when."

When he opened the door, he looked over his shoulder. He could not resist ogling the voluptuous, warm, friendly body. He thought, "I better get out of here." He sprinted to his truck.

Chapter 47

Two days later, late morning, Jeff took the plunge.

"Carl, you up? I didn't wake you? Good. I thought I'd drop by late this afternoon. I got my hands on some good dope. I'll share it with you. You can reimburse me later on, whenever you can."

"Sure, sure, honk when you get here."

The three ladies exited Jeff's truck. Carl smiled, combed his hair with both hands, picked up his pants, and tugged upward on his belt. Jeff walked over to the fence and spoke very softly.

"Here's the weed I talked about. Oh, you like my friends? Ha, ha, you haven't changed."

Carl touched Jeff's shoulder.

"Why don't you all stay? We can get high together."

"No, not today. We have a few things to do. I don't mess around with the girls. A little too young for me. More of your son's age. But if you like younger women, that's cool."

Carl's shoulders slumped as he turned to walk away.

"Carl, wait. You're my buddy. Let me know when Stevie is here visiting, maybe even with a friend. I'll come over with all the girls. We can party then. What do you think?"

Carl's broad smile showed his dark brown teeth and inflamed gums.

"Yeah, make sure you bring all three with you."

Chapter 48

A week later, Carl called Jeff.

"I talked to Stevie last night. He and his friend Joe are coming by Friday afternoon, about five. They'll probably crash here. Can you get the girls to come by?"

"I'll see what I can do." Jeff did not want to put anyone in harm's way. This guy, Carl, scared him. He had to devise a plan that minimized the possibility of collateral damage. He picked up the phone.

"Ben, can we get together alone? Today?"

Chapter 49

Ben told his secretary to go home early. The meeting would be tense. He locked the outer door to his office and put the phones on hold. His veins popped out above his forehead.

"You've gone too far—I should have known better. You're like a cat with catnip. You're thinking of putting three girls in jeopardy. We're dealing with animals who've already killed a young lady. Do you want blood on your hands?"

"Listen, Ben, if I go there alone, I've lost my credibility. It may be easier to take only one girl with me, but it's probably safer as a group. I won't let any of them wander away alone, especially at night. Plus, if I bring all three, the odds are better that one of them will get the guy she's high with, to say something. Anyway, I'll leave it up to the girls."

"Did you say high? Now you're supplying dope to these creatures? If Sally found out, she'd cut your balls off before you went back to prison!"

"Come on, amigo, you got me into this shit. You're right. I'm a dog with a bone. I'm going forward. I'll be…careful."

Jeff drove away. Ben slapped the side of his face three times and moaned.

"What the fuck have I started?"

Chapter 50

"Girls, listen carefully to what I'm going to tell you, and let me know what you think. Here's what's happening."

Suzie, Joyce, and Tina's eyes got wider and wider as he spoke. Joyce drank two stiff drinks during the ten-minute presentation, while Suzie just sucked on her cigarettes. After a few minutes of fidgeting, she started puffing on a reefer.

"That's it. We're in this, all of us, or none of us. It's dangerous to have anyone knowing about this shit while actually not doing it, if you know what I mean."

He did not expect silence from the normally loquacious young ladies. Each appeared stunned and looked at the others for guidance, a cue, a signal, anything to help her cope with the mystery and dilemma laid on her lap by a friend. The drinking, smoking, and puffing continued. He stood up after a while and spoke to no one in particular.

"What the hell am I doing? I'm such an asshole. Please forget all the shit I just told you, and never, and I mean never, bring it up again." He walked toward the door of the double-wide trailer.

Tina yelled. "Jeff, where the fuck do you think you're going? I'm in. Anything I can do to put those cocks in prison for what they did to that poor girl. I'll do anything." She smiled. "Well, not anything unless he is really cute, treats me right, and the dope is good."

Joyce spoke, "Well, I can handle anything. I'm older, been around the block. I'm just concerned about these two, especially Suzie. She's a little, naïve—believes everything that people tell her."

Tina chimed in. "Joyce is right. Just us two will do it. Too dangerous for her. What, twenty-two years old—never been married?"

Suzie stood up, stared around the room, and then broke down with a torrid of tears. She grabbed both her friends.

"You two are the only real family I have ever had. If anything ever happened to either of you and I was not there? No fucking way. I'm part of the scene."

Jeff knew that he only really needed Suzie, the youngest and cutest of the group. Stevie would never be able to resist her. He put both arms to his sides as if he were giving a sermon to his flock.

"Are you sure, Suzie?"

"I'm sure. Let's do it."

He nodded and thought. "Now comes the hard part."

Chapter 51

After several hours of deep reflection and stiff drinks, Jeff believed that he had a good plan. But he had to sleep on it. During the night, his ideas would either marinate to perfection as he tossed, turned, and ground his teeth, or turn to chaotic shit by morning. He crawled out of bed, massaged his sore temples, and stumbled to the kitchen. He admired the desert flowers as he sipped on his hot coffee. Eventually, he felt confident enough to make the call.

"Ben, you awake? Listen to what I have. It should only take a few minutes."

Ben concentrated and focused on every word. His cynical mind accepted the proposed orchestrated sequence of events that seemed well thought out.

"But, still, what happens if one of the girls gets separated from the group and is alone with one of these scumbags?"

Jeff drained his cafe latte. "I'm going to link up each girl with the guy I know she can handle. Look, these guys will be high and horny. They'll take any of these ladies, especially Carl. After a little socialization, I'll figure it out. I'll clue the girls into which guy they should latch onto. I'm pretty sure that I know already how things are going to shake out." He heard a moan on the other side of the phone.

"Oh, Jesus. Please be careful. Keep me informed." His hand trembled as he put down the phone.

Chapter 52

Jeff looked around the Spartan living room as he dragged on his joint. A few tequilas down his throat didn't hurt either. He liked what he saw. Carl kept tugging up his dirty jeans to try to hide the crack of his butt. He laughed to himself and thought what a great plumber Carl would have made.

Little Stevie, short, skinny, with beady eyes and long dirty hair. He wore a checkered long-sleeved shirt that smelled bad. The cowboy hat he wore was too big for his narrow, shallow head.

Joe, the third guy, concerned him. Tall, muscular, tattooed up. Actually, very good-looking if you didn't get freaked out by his piercing, lifeless, cold blue eyes. Long black hair, big hands and forearms, he wore Army-issued camouflage khakis and shirt.

Jeff was satisfied with the decisions he had made and the matchups he had orchestrated. He cleverly guided each lady to the target. Joyce was perfect for Carl. She would show some cleavage, get him to brag about himself, and mention Joy Tweet only if the time was right.

Young, cutie pie Suzie was a perfect match for Stevie, a weakling who would melt if you made him feel bad. She would get him high, make him feel comfortable, and possibly spill some beans.

The third matchup concerned him. But Tina was clever and experienced. A lot of street smarts for only being twenty-six. As long as she kept Joe part of the group, occupied and away from Stevie, things would work out. A short time later, Jeff shook his head and scolded himself for drinking too much and for dozing off. He had to piss. Could not hold it in. He walked to the bathroom, urinated like a racehorse, studied himself in the mirror, tried to clean up a little, and returned to an empty room.

"Where the fuck did everyone go?"

A cold sweat gathered on his forehead. He swung open the door. The sun was low on the horizon. It would be dark soon. He stumbled down the wooden staircase and narrowly missed crashing into Carl and Joyce, who were pointing upward at a few stars slowly emerging. They looked like a normal couple enjoying the stellar beauty descending upon them. Jeff wiped away the marijuana residue from his mouth. He yelled. "Where did Suzie and Tina go?"

Carl frowned, "Don't sweat it. They'll be fine. Stevie borrowed my truck. He and Suzie went to buy more beer."

"What about Tina? She with Joe?"

Carl got in Jeff's face. "They just took a little stroll." He chuckled. "You know how the younger generation is. They cut to the chase faster than we old guys."

Before he had a chance to react, Jeff heard a loud voice, almost a scream behind him. He recognized Tina's voice.

"Listen, I'm going home. I've had enough of this shit."

Two figures emerged from the dusk. She ran to Jeff's side.

"Let's go. It's late." She looked around. "Where's Suzie?"

The large camouflaged figure spoke. "He'll be right back. Just getting more beer and maybe some tequilas."

Jeff concentrated on the hulk. "Well, we're not going without her." He clenched his fists.

Carl chimed in. "Listen, why do you have to be such an old maid?" He smiled at Joyce. "Hell, Joyce and I are starting to get to know one another." He chuckled.

Jeff sensed that neither man was going to back down. He had to show his huevos.

He turned to the less ominous man. "As soon as Suzie comes back, we're out of here."

Joe bumped Jeff with his chest and rolled up his sleeves. The sound of pea gravel being crushed interrupted the eruption that was brewing. Suzie jumped out of the truck and ran toward them.

"Hey, guys, cut it out. Stevie showed me some desert I hadn't seen before. We bought two cases of beer, cans, and bottles."

She turned to Stevie who smiled. "Yeah, what's going on? I'm sorry we took so long."

Tina faced her friend. "I'm tired. Let's hit the road. Suzie?"

The young blonde shrugged, kissed Stevie on the cheek, and said loud enough for all to hear. "I had a great time. Call me, Stevie."

When the truck began to leave, Joe picked up a bottle of Bud and threw it at the back window of the vehicle. The bottle missed its target and exploded in many pieces within the confines of the six-foot bed.

Suzie bellowed at her companions. "What the hell happened back there?"

Jeff kept his eyes on the dark, potholed road.

"I'm too drunk to think about this shit right now. I'll come to your place tomorrow, and we'll talk."

The bright headlights illuminated a coyote staring at them from the wash.

Chapter 53

It was unusually cool that late morning considering the time of year.

"Hey girls, where do we go from here?"

Tina roared: "Fuck all this shit! That guy choked me before I stomped on his foot and ran away. No, no. I'm out of it."

Joyce quietly said. "You know, Carl is not that bad of a guy. But he's too old. I'm not attracted to him. Other than bragging about himself, he doesn't say much. I asked if he lived with a woman or had a girlfriend recently, but he changed the subject right away. Jeff, I don't think your plan is going to work."

Jeff looked down at his shoes. "You know me. I hate to lose at anything. Screw it, we've tried."

As he approached the door, Suzie spoke up.

"Wait. I hate being a spy against Stevie. He's not mean, at least not to me. He is sweet, sensitive, shy. I can't believe he did anything to harm that lady. I asked if his dad had any women friends or dated anyone. He just got real quiet. Then he said that he didn't want to talk about that. He treated me nice. I'd see him again if he asked. We had some fun together."

Jeff's ears perked up. He almost felt guilty about what he needed to set in motion.

Chapter 54

On their third "date," Suzie picked the fuzz and other debris from her butt after sitting on the dreary, moist couch in the rundown apartment. She asked, "Stevie, do you want me to clean this place up? I've got some cleaning products in my trailer. It wouldn't look so bad here with a little effort."

He handed her a beer from the refrigerator. "You don't like this place? My dad warned me that you'd start telling me how to live my life."

"Come on now. For you and Joe it may be livable. No woman could handle the clutter and the dust. Geez, my allergies are starting to bother me again."

"You're right. I'll help. Just don't go into Joe's room. He's real protective of his stuff in there."

"We'll do a little today. When I come back tomorrow, I'll do the real cleaning that it needs."

He gently touched her shoulder. "Why are you doing this? Why do you care?"

She smiled at him. "Stevie, I have feelings for you. Plus, there's no way I could ever stay in a place like this overnight, with or without your roommate."

The next hour together was surreal for both. She had never tidied up for a man. He had never met a female, other than his mother who abandoned him, that ever expressed any affection toward him. She looked in the dark closet and pulled out a used baseball bat with the Louisville Slugger logo on it. She wondered out loud.

"Who's the baseball player? You or Joe?"

Steve ran from the kitchen. "No, no, leave that alone. It's Joe's. I'll put it in his room. He used to be a good baseball player before things turned bad for him."

Ten minutes later, she opened up the greasy, grimy medicine chest and gazed at the used syringe. "And this?" She pointed to the instrument of death. He immediately slammed it shut.

"Please, don't say anything to Joe about this. He's got some problems. But he's my friend, and we work together—landscaping."

The front door opened. Joe stared at Stevie. "Why is she here? What are you two doing?"

"No sweat, Joe. We're just cleaning up the place a little. Suzie's coming back tomorrow to do more with some products. She even has a small vacuum cleaner."

The larger man turned toward her as he opened up the refrigerator door.

"Stay out of my room. Hey, how's Tina doing? She's got a great ass!" He laughed before slugging down the bottle of pale ale.

Suzie crossed her arms. "Well, you'll never see that ass again!"

He gave her the finger. "Well, fuck you and your big-titted friend!"

Stevie squeaked out a few words. "Joe, she's my guest."

Joe shook his head with condescension and disdain, walked into his dusty, smelly, lifeless cave, and slammed the door.

Chapter 55

Joe Davis, aka "the perv," by his closest associates, grabbed the Louisville Slugger with Mickey Mantle's signature on it that leaned against the wall next to the unkempt bed. The brown sheets originally were white. His brain was inflamed as he thought. "That snoopy bitch must have seen it in the closet. That dumb fucking runt. I'll kill both of them if he tells her anything. I'll use this like I did with that skinny moron Joy."

He briefly recalled better days when he was getting noticed by colleges for his baseball skills. His anger quickly erupted and wiped away any pleasant memories.

"That Jew coach didn't play me my senior year. He played that spic Carlos ahead of me. Then he put me in as a pinch runner and told me to knock the ball out of the catcher's hands."

He rubbed the left knee that was heavily laden with metal.

"It was his fault—that day my world ended."

He drained the bottle of ale and threw it hard against the door. He hoped that the wimpy roommate and the dumb blonde would get scared and leave.

Chapter 56

Suzie thought that her decision would be final. She needed to tell Jeff that all her snooping was over. She cared about Stevie. Her deception was tearing her up inside. But he was relentless.

"You asked what happened to Joy and he put his head down and cried? You saw a bat and a syringe? He told you that his dad put new tires on the old truck?"

She nodded and sipped on a cherry-flavored wine cooler.

"Suzie, we need the bat and the syringe. Probably DNA on them. You can do it. You've penetrated this young man's soul. He'll open up more if you push a little harder."

Suzie looked out the window and whispered. "Oh, Stevie." She turned to face him. "And what about that monster Joe? He'll crush me like a cockroach."

Jeff studied the black bug slowly traversing above her head on the ceiling.

"OK Stay put for a while. Don't go back to the apartment. I'll report to Ben, lay it all out for him. Probably not enough to get a search warrant. I'll call you in a few days."

When Suzie heard the screeching of the truck's tires tearing up the soft gravel, she rolled herself a joint, took a few drags, and closed her eyes. She needed sleep, serenity, peace, and some time for her brain to slow down.

Chapter 57

Ben Russo went down memory lane as he awaited Jeff's arrival. What strange things have happened in his life? He had not seen the little man with bumblebee wings for a long time. He would never forget the energy of his presence. Thankfully, he had not needed the assistance of his winged friend for over a decade. But this Joy Tweet thing. Who knows what could happen? His phone buzzed. He told his secretary to let him in.

"Here's the deal, Ben."

The counselor was never good at hiding his thoughts. The perplexed look on his face gave him away. Jeff grimaced.

"So you don't like my plan?"

Ben reached for his bottle. It was almost 5 pm. "Do you want a drink?"

"Not for me. I need to think clearly."

"Well, think about this. You're needlessly putting this Suzie girl in danger with no backup. No, no, no. We have to do it in a different way."

Jeff leaned back. "I'll have that drink now. What do you suggest?"

Ben circled the room for almost a minute, looked out the window, and completely drained his glass. He sat down in a heap with one hand on his forehead.

"I guess it is unavoidable. You're right. The key to open the flood gates is to break down this kid Stevie. But what if he panics, somehow gets his friend involved? She'll be up the creek with no paddle."

Jeff frowned. "Cut out the clichés. Help me out here."

Ben pointed. "You and I have to be there when she talks to Stevie. She'll be the good cop, and we'll be the bad cops. We'll explain the upside of cooperating with us. Even if he freaks out, nothing bad can happen to her if we're there."

Jeff pounded his glass on the desk and grabbed the bottle.

"Your plan sucks, will not work. He'll never say anything if we're there. Suzie, alone, in her own way, has to get him to spill his guts. Fuck, you lawyers think you know everything."

Both men felt the effects of the Canadian Club whiskey. Subtlety no longer existed. Ben nodded.

"OK, let's run this by Suzie. She'll talk to him alone, in her trailer, wear something sexy to keep him interested. She needs to get to know him better before they get any closer, if you know what I mean. She'll find a way to ask about Joy. Can't be too pushy, or he'll smell a rat. Sorry about the cliché. She'll call us, pretend that her mother is on the phone. We'll rush in and take it from there. What do you think? You said that she is smart? Can she carry the ball?"

Jeff smirked as he finished his third whiskey.

"It can work. It has to work."

Chapter 58

Joe grabbed the back of Carl's shirt and turned him around. The older man threw up his hands.

"What the fuck do you want?"

"Your midget runt son is hanging out with that whore Suzie. I saw them together at the apartment a few days ago."

"So what? Maybe the little dick will get laid one of these days instead of jerking off in front of you!"

"Listen, asshole, the bat was in my room, not in the closet where I put it. Someone snooped around in the bathroom, maybe found the hypodermic needle. He's letting her clean the apartment. What is he going to let her do or tell her when he gets in her pants? I've warned him."

The older man shrugged his shoulders. "Oh, you worry too much. Stevie would never snitch on anyone. Maybe you should have thought about that before you drugged the dumb bitch and slaughtered her with your Louisville Slugger!"

The younger man jumped on him, knocked him to the ground, and held his arms down. The spittle sprayed from his mouth as he shouted. "I'm not going to prison for the rest of my life because of that crazy slut you were trying to get rid of. I did your dirty work. Shit got out of hand. You're fucked too. What about the bloody blanket you burned up and the tires you threw away? You're in this shit up to your eyeballs!"

The other man looked up and mumbled through the hands around his throat.

"I protected my son. He'd never make it in prison."

The hands loosened. He got up and patted the dust off his shoulders and jeans.

"What do you want me to do?"

The young man's eyes were those of a hawk slowly devouring its prey. "Tell Stevie to keep his mouth shut or he and his blonde whore will be taken care of by the Slugger. Do you understand?"

"Sure, sure, as soon as I see him."

Chapter 59

Suzie had never before allowed him to have sexual intercourse with her, but she knew that she had pleased him in the past. Her searching hands had often caused him to vibrate and climax under his jeans. But this time was different. She was more physically and emotionally attracted to him, despite his childish awkwardness. She whispered in his ear. "Stevie, we're going to make love. I know that you want it—me too. But you'll stay and we'll talk afterward?"

He barely uttered the words, "Sure, OK," as she adroitly caressed his whole body. She massaged his extended manhood and gently mounted the man/boy beneath her. He soon jerked and spasmed. She kissed his ear.

"It's all right, sweetie. Rest up awhile. We'll do it again. It will be better, for both of us, the second time around."

She lit a reefer, took two long drags, and handed it to him. He stared at the ceiling and prayed that she would never leave him. The time was right for her to complete her mission.

"Stevie, honey, I need to know something before we go any further. It's important to me."

He breathed hard and turned to her. "What's that?"

Her tongue traversed his chest and her hand cradled his recovering organ.

"What happened to Joy Tweet?"

Chapter 60

Suzie listened to his snoring. She smiled and was proud. He earned the pleasure she had given him. After all, he had spit out his guts to her. She reached for the phone. "Hello, come on over. He's asleep."

The other voice was loud. "What have you been doing? Ben and I waited in the hot sun for two hours!"

"Just come, now."

She turned around. His eyes were wide as he sat up.

"Who did you call? Who was that on the phone?"

"Oh, my mother. She asked me to babysit my sister's kid tomorrow."

"Bullshit! That was a man's voice. Are you going to turn me in? My dad and Joe warned me about you!"

"Oh, come on, honey. I would never do that."

He pounced up, shook her shoulders, and pushed her head into the wall. He heard a noise. Two men rushed in. The younger one kicked him in the back of his legs and knocked him down.

"Leave her alone, you fucking murderer!"

The pained boy/man looked up. "Murderer? I'm no murderer." He looked at Suzie. "Tell him. Tell them."

She rubbed the back of her head and twisted her neck.

"Yes, he's an immature asshole, not worthy of me, but not a murderer. He's afraid of that monster Joe and loyal to his brain-dead father. Talk to him, Jeff. Let him know what you can do for him."

Jeff turned to Ben. "Do your thing, abogado."

Ben kneeled down next to the prostrate young man whose face expressed anger, fear, and reconciliation. "Look, son, you're not much older than my daughters. You've protected your friend and father. I understand. But I can help you, hopefully, keep you out of prison. Get this all behind you. Do you want me to try to do that for you?"

The boy cried and put his hands over his eyes.

"I didn't know. He said that he'd give her some drugs and that she'd have sex…with both of us. She said no. He went crazy. He kept punching her, kicking her. The blood, the screaming. She got quiet. He told me to help him carry her into the desert, off the side of the road. We left her in the dirt. She moaned. We walked back to the truck. Then he took his bat from the back seat and ran. I yelled, 'No, no, Joe, leave her alone.' In a few minutes, he came back. His clothes were wet with blood. He used a blanket to dry off the blood in the truck."

He turned to Ben and grabbed his arm. "Can you help me?"

Chapter 61

Joe pointed his rifle. "Where do you think you all are going?"

The group of four stopped and stared at one another. One spoke up.

"Joe, dad, I didn't say anything." He felt the rifle in his chest.

"Oh, sure, you didn't, you little punk snitch. Carl, tie them all up. Here're the rope and knife."

The older man put his pistol in his back pocket and tied up Jeff, Ben, and Suzie, behind their backs, using all the skills learned from his Navy service. When he got to Stevie, he turned to Joe.

"We can trust Stevie. He won't run away."

"No, no, old man. Tie him up. We'll deal with him later."

The father said to his son, "Sorry, I have to do this."

Joe yelled. "Here, take this electrical tape. Put it on their stinking mouths."

The prisoners were thrown into the back of the old VW bus that Joe had borrowed from one of his drug-dealing buddies. As he began to drive away, Carl in the front seat asked, "Now, what are you going to do?"

The driver's eyes dug deeply into the older man's face. "Just turn around, point the rifle at them. If anyone moves an inch, kill all of them."

Ben could see through the small solitary window in the back. They were going deep into the desert, west of the city. They passed the exits to Old Tucson and the Arizona-Sonora Desert Museum. He thought, "We're on dirt side roads. No one will find our bodies out here, not in these hills."

Jeff heard the gravel, dirt, and sound of the occasional pothole under the thin, shallow bottom of the vehicle. He mentally assessed the situation.

"We're fucked. He'll stop soon. I have to do something. Maybe I can at least save Suzie. I got her involved in this shit."

The old vehicle, twisting and turning over roads rarely used, slowed to a stop. Joe turned to Carl. "Get them out. Have them kneel at the rear of the van, on their knees."

The older man did not move. Joe pointed a pistol at Stevie in the back.

"Carl, I'll kill him right now if you fuck with me in any way. I haven't decided yet what to do with your faggot little boy. Now move it if you want to save his skinny ass!"

The sunset dazzled that early evening. Wisps of green, blue, and purple filled the horizon. Ben admired the rainbow colors. His knees, back, and shoulders hurt as he kneeled helplessly on the gravel and dirt.

Suzie whimpered. Stevie's blotchy red face contorted as he struggled with his mouth and tongue to remove the tape. Joe exited the van holding a rifle in one hand and the Louisville Slugger in the other. He stared at his prey and smirked at Stevie as he wiggled the bat. The boy/man somehow created some space between his lips. He muttered. "Dad, save me. Save us."

The shoulders of the older man paralyzed with fear and indecision slumped down as he stared at the ground. Joe walked over to Ben, ripped off the tape over his parched mouth, and placed the front of the rifle directly over his left temple.

"You're going to get it first, asshole. I figured it was you, you fucking mouthpiece scumbag, who started all of this nosying into my business. You got anything to say before your brains color the desert red? Beg, motherfucker, beg!"

Ben decided to pray, make it right, talk to God before he died. Maybe he'd see his deceased parents again. He bent his head downward. His words were barely audible. "My Lord and God, I am truly sorry for all the sins I have committed. I now acknowledge my love for You, before my death, and ask for your heavenly forgiveness."

The young man with the rifle looked at him with disdain and said for all to hear. "What a pussy."

Ben opened his eyes when he heard the sound of the bullet being chambered. Were his eyes deceiving him? He thought, "It's been so long. Will it happen again?"

A vision, an essence, an energy, a translucent man with bumblebee wings descended. The force knocked the rifle out of the evil one's hands into a deep thicket of jumping cacti. Joe yelled. "What the fuck is going on?" He took the Slugger with both hands, raised it above his head, and prepared to crush the head below him into red Jell-O. His arms stiffened and tightened. The bat fell out of his hands. He lifted one booted foot and smashed it into the praying man's stomach. He raised the boot again ready to pulverize the back of the groaning man's head against the desert floor.

A voice. "No, Joe, this has gone too far."

Va voom! The sound of the 9-mm pistol startled and scattered the surrounding desert life preparing to rest for the evening. The bullet struck the left side of Joe's chest and spun him around before his face thumped into the hard ground. The shooter threw the pistol down, ran to his son, hugged him, and spoke through his tears. "Please forgive me. I was not much of a father to you after your mother…left. I couldn't let this happen to you." His head caved into the son's face and neck.

"It's OK, Dad. We're in this together—like family. It will work out. I love you."

Chapter 62

Carl and Stevie released Ben, Suzie, and Jeff from their constraints. Ben looked at the others. "Did you see what I saw? Was it a man, a bird—bumblebee wings? What the hell was that?"

Jeff spoke first. "My eyes were closed. I didn't see anything."

The confused abogado turned to Suzie and Stevie. Their embrace melded them into one. They said. "Same here."

The cynical attorney was not convinced. "Carl, you must have seen it, didn't you?"

He shrugged his shoulders. "Counselor, I have no idea what you're talking about."

It was silent in the darkening desert. Jeff took over.

"Let's get out of here. It'll soon be pitch black. Anybody know how to get back to town?"

Stevie released Suzie from his hug. "I know where we are. I'll drive." He stared at the carcass on the ground. "That prick and I have been out here many times, mostly shooting our pistols. Help me, guys, load this piece of shit in the back."

The van's bright lights pointed in the direction of the vast, broad illumination on the horizon. Ben tried to understand, to rationalize what had happened. What was real? Was it a hallucination? His brain could not accept either conclusion. He wondered. "Can the same illusion occur over and over again? Is that possible? But then again…"

Chapter 63

Ben often cited the expression "all's well that ends well." But what a torturous and treacherous journey. The trial prosecutor was euphoric that the murder case had been solved. He called a press conference and more than implied that he had single-handedly orchestrated the result. At Ben's incessant urging, he offered extremely lenient plea agreements. Ruth Tweet gave her blessing to the stipulated punishments. All she ever wanted was to find out how and why her only child died.

Carl served five years in prison, a fraction of what the sentencing guidelines prescribed. Stevie spent a year in the county jail as a condition of his probation. He earned a GED and took every available Bible class. Suzie visited him every weekend and remained loyal during his confinement. During the day, she worked at Macy's selling cosmetics. At night, she studied at the community college toward obtaining her nursing degree. She abstained from smoking weed.

Jeff's girlfriend, Sally, evicted him from her home. She resented his smoking dope with three young females and the facade he had presented to her. Jeff cried and begged for three months before she took him back.

Ben's wife interrogated him about the details of his playing Sherlock Holmes. As a result, he was relocated to his daughter's bedroom until Christmas break. He couldn't count the number of times he said "yes, dear." He agonized over the tragic death of Joy Tweet. Although he believed in God, he could not help questioning. "Why, Lord, do you let horrible things happen to good people? I'm not filled with enough of your grace to understand. Please help me."

He recited the same prayer every night. "Please, Lord, say hello to my parents. Tell them I love and miss them and that I hope to see them someday. Also, give my love to Joy, who has been absorbed into your eternal kingdom. May they rest in peace."

Chapter 64

30 May 2010, Benson, Arizona

Jorge Verdugo, late-night shift, driving to the power plant. He lights up in order to relax. Late for work. The guy in front of him is driving like a snail. He moves to pass on the left and accelerates his Ford 150 pickup as he drops the joint on the floorboard. "Oh, fuck." He reaches down to pick it up.

"Boom!"

Two vehicles crashed together, like accordions. His head impales into the steering wheel and dashboard.

Two weeks later Jorge wakes up, alive, a survivor. His family's lawyer informs him that three men died in the other vehicle. Two police officers impatiently pace outside the room. The head nurse angrily shoos them away.

Chapter 65

20 April 2011, Bisbee, Arizona

Sixty-eight-year-old Luis Armenta threw down his jacket and glared at the thirty-year-old Cochise County prosecutor who receded deeper behind his small desk piled high with thick files.

"Mr. Nelson, you offered probation to the drugged-out animal who killed my son, Frank, destroyed my life, his mother's life, and the lives of his wife and children? What kind of justice is this?"

"Sir, Senor Armenta, my superiors in this office, the people I take directions from, agreed to the deal of involuntary manslaughter. The Judge can send the defendant to prison or give him probation. He comes from a good family, well known for their grocery business, the good deeds they have done for the county, and the charities they are involved in. His attorney, very experienced and respected, made some good arguments. The facts show more of an accident than an intentional or reckless criminal act. He's never been in trouble before. The marijuana had no effect on his sobriety. It could have been a cell phone or a cigarette."

Peter Nelson kept his distance behind the desk. When Luis went left, he went right. The other man's eyes pierced his chest.

"You *pinche*, fucking white boy! Are you loco? Three young men died. You're giving this *pendejo* a chance to go free?"

Peter's red blotched face twitched. His shaking hand picked up the phone, and he whispered to his paralegal.

"Brenda. Is Joe Ferguson in the office? I need his help. Please get him."

Chapter 66

1 May 2011, Tucson, Arizona

Luis Armenta put down his fourth beer on the bar after hearing the ring and looking at the small screen.

"Yes, Josie, what do you want?"

"When are you coming home? It's 7:30. Where are you? Are you bringing back the groceries I asked you to get?"

He picked up his can of beer. "They're in the truck. Just having a few beers at the VFW. I'll be home soon."

"You sound tired. Are you OK? Come home. I'll heat up the food."

He shut his eyes. He felt a strong hand on his shoulder and heard a raspy, slurred, heavily accented voice.

"Hey, what's up, Luis? You don't look too good—remember me? The new guy installed last week. Afghanistan vet, Rafael Cisneros."

"Oh, hi, Rafael—I'm OK. Just got a lot of shit on my mind. Got to go home, anyway."

"*Digame*, amigo. I've got time on my hands. My *novia* is not here. Susanna lives in Hermosillo. I'm trying to figure out how to get her up here. Come on, I'm a friend. Talk to me, *hombre*."

Luis finished his beer and ordered and paid for two more.

"Rafael, do you know what happened to my son, Frank, about a year ago?"

"Not much. A car accident, and other guys died too? I'm really sorry, Luis."

"A wife without a husband. Two kids without a father. Only thirty years old. He was on his way back to Tucson after hunting in the Dragoon Mountains. Some fucking doper crashed into his vehicle. He was the front passenger. The driver and the guy in the back died too."

"Fuck! What *pendejo* did this? Does he live around here?"

"Nope. The puto lives in Benson. The prosecutor is going to let him go. No prison. He sees the Judge in June."

Luis pounded his beer on the bar and put one hand over his eyes. He tried to speak through his tears.

"What did you say, amigo? I couldn't hear you."

"May 30th. This month. It will be one year since my boy died."

The young burly man with the barrel chest clenched both fists, slugged down his beer, and ordered two more.

"Don't worry, *viejo*. I'll help you."

"Help me?" He laughed. "What are you talking about? What can you do?"

The other man stuck out his chest. "I know what to do. You said, Benson? How far is that from here?"

Chapter 67

The man in the camouflaged outfit, mask, and hoodie turned off the Jeep's lights and parked off the side of the dirt road. Almost light outside. He could barely see the old, small wooden house one hundred yards away. He closed his eyes and made the sign of the cross.

"I have to do this. Make it right for Luis. This *pendejo* is going to pay for what he did."

He loaded his 9 mm. "Just in case." He placed it in his back pocket, tightly grasped the baseball bat and crowbar, and quietly traversed the trail leading to his destination. He completed his reconnaissance the week before. No dogs or pesky neighbors walking in the early morning. He adroitly broke open the latch to the back door. No sound. A smattering of light from the outside. The door to the bedroom was open. He low crawled the last several yards. The bat in the right gloved hand. The crowbar in the left. He heard a gentle snoring as he laid the crowbar on the carpeted floor. He thought, "I'll whack this puto on the legs and the back of the *cabeza*. A bad headache, maybe some broken bones. He deserves it."

He stood up and saw a body covered up by a white sheet. The bat held in his two strong hands smashed twice onto the back of the legs. A scream and a groan. The head popped up from under the pillow. The assailant blurted out.

"What the fuck!"

The female screamed, "Jorge!"

The hands and fists of a third person in his underwear grabbed and punched the back of the intruder's head and tore off his mask. He shouted. "Who are you? What are you doing here?"

No option. He was compromised. His instincts took over. He grabbed the 9 mm. First the man in the temple. Then the woman in the back of the head.

Chapter 68

4 June 2011, Tucson

Luis enjoyed reading the Daily Star, especially the sports pages. He'd skim the rest to see if anything caught his eye. Not interested in politics, but it gave him a pleasure to read about the heroics of his fellow combat veterans. He was quietly proud of the Bronze Star for valor awarded for his service as a Marine in Viet Nam. As he began to crumble up the paper, he noticed the heading of an article.

"Man and woman found dead in Benson."

His face turned red and then purple as he read:

> The Cochise County Sheriff's Office, as a result of a call from a neighbor who heard two shots, searched a Benson home and found the deceased bodies of a man and a woman. An unnamed source indicated that the victims, Jorge Verdugo and Gloria Lopez, each died from a single gunshot wound. No other information is available at this time.

He felt faint and staggered to the couch in his living room. His head pounded. His temples quivered. His jaw tightened. He threw up. The voice in his head would not stop talking. "Oh, God, oh my God, what have I done?"

Chapter 69

9 am

He pounded on the door of the VFW. He heard a noise inside. "Open up! Open up!"

The seventy-six-year-old groggy gentleman slowly opened the door. "Luis, why are you making so much noise? You're lucky that I'm here. I slept in the office. You know this place does not open up till noon."

"I need the membership list. All members. Phone numbers, addresses. Now!"

"Why would I give you that information? It's supposed to be confidential."

"Jim, I've known you for thirty years. I can't tell you why now. Maybe someday. Please."

The older man stared at the disheveled figure who normally was impeccably dressed and groomed.

"Fuck it. Only this one time. No one can find out about this. We could get our asses thrown out of the lodge."

His search was futile. The man disappeared a few days ago. All of his clothes were gone. No forwarding address. He even left a returnable deposit for his apartment. The disinterested landlord spoke to him.

"Mr. Cisneros must have left in his Jeep. I haven't seen it. Check with the Border Patrol. He's probably in Mexico by now. I never did like him. The foreign music he played was loud and obnoxious. The neighbors complained."

Chapter 70

1 October 2011, Tucson

Ben Russo, six months short of his 72nd birthday, looked out the window and admired the beginning of a multi-colored sunset. All alone, he was ready to go home. His secretary, Kathy, left early to celebrate her daughter's birthday party at school. A knock on the door. He put down the bottle of whiskey he was about to pour.

"Who is it?" He opened the door. A well-dressed Hispanic man wearing a cowboy hat took it off and stuck out his hand.

"Sir, I don't have an appointment, but I need help. My name is Raul Verdugo."

Ben glanced at the bottle and his watch before he looked at the anguished face before him. "Mr. Verdugo—can I call you Raul? You probably do not know this, but I've decided to retire in the next few months, hopefully by the end of the year." He smiled. "You know, enough is enough. I'm going to finish up the cases I already have and not take on any new work."

The anguish elevated to confusion and desperation.

"You represented a friend of mine a long time ago. He said that you could explain things to me—maybe help me find out who killed my son Jorge and his girlfriend, Gloria Lopez. She was five months pregnant—would have been my first grandchild."

Ben slumped to his chair. "Raul, please sit down. Please sit down. I have a few minutes. Who is this friend of yours?"

"Ralph Ortiz. Do you remember him? He is about your age. Tall, mustache, darker than me."

"Ralph? Great guy. He's sent me many clients over the years. How's he doing?"

"Well, not too good. He has stomach cancer. But about my son. Can I explain why I'm here?"

Ben thought. "I told the boss lady that I'd be home by six."

"OK, Senor. I'll listen, but I can't make any promises."

Chapter 71

1 October 2011, Tucson

Ben did not say much when he got home at 7:00 and devoured the dinner left on the table by his wife, Jennifer. After all these years, she still cooked for him even though he often came home late. She appreciated that he placed his dishes in the dishwasher before turning on the news. That night, he was unusually quiet and did not turn on the TV.

"What's the matter, Ben? Had a bad day at work? Only a few months to go. You won't have to deal with the crazies anymore."

She put on the news and listened to the latest news of an unarmed man being shot and killed and the ensuing racial protest. Then a report concerning the arrest of a Neo-Nazi planning to blow up a synagogue filled with children training for their Bar Mitzvahs.

"Ben, you have to see this sick thing in handcuffs pretending to be a human being."

He shrugged his shoulder. "I'm tired. I have to make a decision that may delay my retirement. Not sure of what to do. I'll have to sleep on it."

"Before you sleep, tell me about it, if you can. I have the time. I called the girls but they were both too busy with the kids." She turned off the TV. "Come on, I'm all ears."

Chapter 72

1 October 2011, Tucson

By the time Ben finished his tale about Raul Verdugo's tragic situation, it was almost 9 pm. "I'm going to bed. I promised Mr. Verdugo that I'd give him my answer tomorrow morning."

"Ben, this man wants you to investigate and find out who killed his son. Why would you agree to do that? You're not the police or a prosecutor."

He nodded. "You're right—but I know that the Benson cops will never put in the time and effort that I could with the right investigator. Plus, I know that the Cochise County prosecutors will have to cooperate if I represent Raul and his family...the victims. They have to talk to me and give me all the police reports."

"I hate to be crass, but are you going to be paid for this? You'll be retired soon. A lot less money coming in."

He flinched. "Everything will be fine. I've got it covered."

She stood up, walked away, and never glanced back. He heard. "Sure you do." He did not hear the other words she mumbled under her breath.

Chapter 73

15 October 2011, Tucson

Tim Phillips smiled when he saw his amigo. "You old goat! How the hell have you been? I haven't heard from you since the Berkman case. You know I've cut down on my workload and am transitioning everything to my son Joe."

"The last several years I have changed my practice to mostly civil work. That's why I haven't needed you. I spend most of my time sucking up to doctors treating my clients. But I was just hired to investigate a criminal matter. A double homicide. I'll have to step on a few toes."

Tim grinned. "Whose toes are we talking about?"

"The Cochise County Sheriff's Office and Attorney's Office."

"They aren't so bad. I have some friends in Bisbee. What's going on?"

After listening for thirty minutes, the man behind the desk spoke. "Two obvious things come to mind. First, we'll be pissing in the wind thinking that we'll do a better job than experienced cops and prosecutors. Second, is your client willing to pay our fees if we come up empty?"

"Don't worry. You'll get paid by me personally."

"OK, I'm in. What's the plan?"

"I'm the victim's attorney. I'll share all the police reports with you. My client and I will sign a letter advising everyone that you have the same authority as me. You'll get a copy of the decedent's indictment and anything else you need."

"Be more specific. What is your gut feeling?"

"I've got no proof, no corroboration, but this is not a random killing of a young man and his pregnant girlfriend. Exactly one year later to the day that Jorge Verdugo killed three men in a car accident, he is shot in the temple. I've never believed in coincidences. These murders were very personal. Listen, just talk to anyone and everyone."

Tim shook the abogado's hand. "OK big spender. Joe will do most of the legwork. If he smells something funny, I'll be on it."

Chapter 74

Joe Phillips was cocky, combative, and stubborn. His father wanted him to become a professional man, maybe a doctor or a CPA, and not get his hands dirty with criminal punks, scumbags, and lawyers. But he never liked school or study or read books about topics he could not care less about. He wanted action. He joined the Navy after high school and ultimately became a decorated Seal. He was forced to leave after a secret deployment on the Afghanistan/Pakistan border. When he found out that a captain in the Afghan Army was raping a twelve-year-old boy, he unmercifully beat the man until several American soldiers managed to pull him off the bloodied, butchered, broken face lying in the dirt.

The Navy said hasta la vista and gave him an honorable discharge with the proviso that he could never again serve in any branch of the military. No charges were ever filed. He missed being a Seal. He even thought of becoming a cop. But he knew that taking orders was not in his DNA. When his money ran out, he put his tail between his legs and humbly asked his dad for a job. Tim knew that if his son could put his temper in check, he would be an asset to the business. He was the talker. Joe would be the muscle. It became a symbiotic relationship.

After reading all of the reports, Joe thought, "Who would have wanted the woman dead? Must be collateral damage. In the wrong place at the wrong time. Two clean shots point-blank with a 9-mm. No fingerprints or witnesses. The perp has to have law enforcement or military experience."

Chapter 75

5 November 2011, Tucson

"Listen, Dad, this is a needle in a haystack. Probably not going anywhere. I talked to everyone. They cooperated. Not hostile. Nothing solid—but one thing lingers in my head. Only a hunch."

"Well, what is it?"

"Luis Armenta, Frank's father. Something in his eyes, in his head. He did not say much. Read my report. He's not telling me all he knows. I just feel it. Anyway, talk to the lawyer. Probably the smart thing for him is to save his money and call off the dogs. I'm sure that he is not going to give a shit about my feeling."

Chapter 76

"Kathy, let Tim in." The door opened.

"Hey, counselor, how have you been? I figured I'd report in before consuming all your dinero."

"What have you got? Are the papers in your hand your report?"

"Maybe nothing in there, but Joe has good instincts. He was trained to study people. He sees things that you and I would not see."

Ben leaned back and closed his eyes. "It's been a long day."

"OK, I'll get to the point. Frank Armenta, a young man with a wife and two young children, died. His dad, Luis, a veteran, grieved horribly, as any father would. Joe saw something in his eyes when he interviewed him."

Ben stood up. "I'm paying you $100.00 per hour for your psychic son to study eyes? How about my bloodshot eyes when I had too much to drink?"

"Hold on. This Luis guy is a gun owner, a VFW member. Everyone in the VFW owns a gun. Maybe he spilled his guts out to other members. They're loyal to each other. Revenge. Maybe he didn't do it, but he knows who did. The cops treated him with kid gloves when they interviewed him. I guess that they did not want to add more pain to the situation. You're a vet. Maybe you should talk to him."

"Tim, what can I do that the cops and Joe did not?"

"You're about the same age as Luis. Also, a fellow Viet Nam vet. Bond with him. Commiserate over his loss. Point out to him that Raul Verdugo is also suffering from the death of his son—his grandchild."

Ben winced. He thought that he should never have gotten involved in this conundrum. "I'll think about it after I read the report. Anything else?"

"A few suggestions from me. Check out the VFW. Talk to some members. The cops never went over there. Have a few beers. Tell your bullshit war stories." He smiled.

Ben shook his head and looked in the direction of his bottle of Irish whiskey. "Nice talking to you, *hombre*."

Chapter 77

After two nights of drinking beer with seventy- and eighty-year-old vets, telling them tall tales, Ben was antsy and bored. Jim, the lodge Commander, said that Luis was a great man who kept to himself but did an enormous amount of community service to homeless vets and charities.

"He never turned down our requests to help people. A hard-working, humble man. We all felt terrible when his son died. But he keeps to himself. I only saw him talk to a new guy once. Rafael Cisneros. I haven't seen him lately. Anyway, Luis usually comes in about 5:30 once or twice a week. He has a few beers by himself and then leaves."

A few days later, Ben looked at his watch and mumbled to himself.

"Six thirty. I'm going home. Jennifer is going to wonder what the hell I've been doing lately."

He got off his stool and waved bye to the bartender. A man in his late sixties, Hispanic, thick mustache, stocky, full head of hair, sat down on a nearby stool. He thought. "Maybe Luis."

He nervously surveyed the room before sitting down next to the man having his first sip of beer.

"How are you doing? I'm Ben, soon to retire. I'm checking out the lodge. I may join. I'll have a lot of time on my hands soon."

The other man barely looked up, managed a tight smile, and stared at the sports announcer on the TV screen.

Ben had to take the plunge. "I think I know your name. You are Luis Armenta? I read about your son, Frank. I'm so sorry for your loss."

The man nodded and took another sip.

"You're a Viet Nam vet?"

"Yeah. So what?"

"I was there too. Army. Mostly Cu Chi. What part of the Nam were you?"

"Da Nang—further north—the marines."

"How rough was it there?"

The man shook his head. "A long time ago. I don't remember much." He motioned to the bartender for another beer. Ben waved to the bartender.

"I'll get that. Two beers."

Ben felt awkward, out of his element. He knew that the marines did most of the fighting in Viet Nam against the North Viet Namese Army. They suffered an enormous amount of casualties taking on well-equipped, trained, dedicated soldiers. Luis was awarded the Bronze Star for valor for his heroism in firefights.

"You're the only marine I ever talked to who served in Viet Nam. I know mostly Army guys. Maybe a few in the Navy. All I encountered were booby traps. No one shot at us. How close were the NVA when you engaged them?"

The Hispanic man grinned, chuckled, and finally acknowledged the white, disheveled, bearded man.

"You really want to hear about this shit? Why?"

"I'm a nosy guy. Like to learn things. Well, anyway, Jim said that I could get involved in helping other vets and their families."

"I'll talk about that. Not the other crap." At 7:30, Luis looked at the clock on the wall. "I have to go, Senor. *Mi esposa* is waiting for me—nice meeting you."

"Luis, can we talk again?"

"I'll be back in a week. *Hasta la proxima, hombre.*"

Chapter 78

21 November 2011, Tucson

"Hello, Tim Phillips."

"Tim, I got a chance to talk to Luis Armenta a few days ago. We had a few beers. A nice humble guy. I did not see any telltale signs in his eyes. I'm conflicted. Maybe I should just leave him alone—I feel guilty pretending to be someone thinking about joining the lodge instead of a lawyer with an agenda that could put him in prison."

"You have to go forward. We checked the name you gave us. Rafael Cisneros—a bad dude originally from Mexico. He crossed the border with his parents when he was a kid. He joined the Army. A paratrooper, ranger, infantry. The whole nine yards. In Afghanistan, he was punished for using his rifle smashing the brains of a Taliban soldier in handcuffs in front of other soldiers. He bragged about it. The Army did not know what to do with him. When the commanding officer tried to counsel him, he told the captain to fuck off and that he'd do it again if given the chance. You know the rest. Honorably discharged and released to the rest of humanity here. Because he was a vet, he received his full citizenship."

"Where is he now?"

"All we know is that within one week of Verdugo's death, Cisneros went to Mexico. His vehicle was found at the Nogales border. The Border Patrol has it in storage. A new, shiny, paid-up Jeep left to rot at the border. Maybe the dots are coming together."

"I'm not an investigator. I've tried to go down memory lane with this guy. He is not a talker. Should I leave this poor soul in peace?"

"Come clean and see what happens. He probably knows where Cisneros is. The Federales are not going to bust their asses looking for him. But if we know his probable location, who knows? I have connections in a few of the cities down there."

Ben frowned when he put down his phone. He thought, "I feel like such a rat. Luis is a good man who served his county well. Here I am setting him up for a major prison term. Fuck, I should never have taken this case."

Chapter 79

Ben went a little earlier than usual to the VFW. He needed extra time to get a little high, settle his nerves, get ready for the tough conversation he expected. An hour later, the short husky man, wearing his hat with VFW on the front and Marine Corp on the back, took his customary stool. Ben picked up his beer, got the bartender's attention, and ordered a beer for Luis and a shot of whiskey for himself.

"Luis, your money is no good here. I've got you covered."

After a few drinks and superficial conversations about football and basketball, they stared at one another. Luis went first.

"You know, I thought that I made a new friend. I spoke with some of the other members about you." His face came closer and changed expression.

"Most thought that you're an undercover cop investigating the lodge for violations. A few said you've asked a lot of questions about me. What's the deal, Senor? Who the fuck are you?" He stood up.

Ben stayed in his seat. "I'm not a cop, but a lawyer who usually defends people charged with crimes. Do you remember talking to Joe Phillips, the investigator?"

Silence.

"I hired Joe. A client retained me to investigate the death of his son. You know who I'm talking about."

"I'm out of here. Like I told that young punk, I know nothing. But you know what? I'm glad that he died. That puto killed my son, left his wife without a husband, his kids without a father. So go to hell—don't bother me again."

Ben spoke softly. "Senor, no disrespect for you or your loss. But this man is also suffering. He lost his son and a grandchild. The young woman was five months pregnant."

151

The dark brown eyes glared. "So why are you fucking with me? Do I look like a murderer?"

The taller man stood up. "You know who killed Jorge and Gloria. Maybe your friend Rafael did it. He fled to Mexico. Luis, you are a good man. Tell me what you know."

The other man slammed his empty glass on the counter and shouted.

"Go to hell, *pendejo*!" He exited the premises.

The bartender approached. "What's your name again? Get the hell out of here. Get lost or I'll call the police."

"OK, OK, but listen. Take my card with my phone number on it. Do me one favor and you'll never see me again."

"What do you want?"

"Give this card to Luis the next time that you see him. Please—do that for me."

The man glanced at the card and placed it in a large glass filled with several others. As Ben walked out, he felt the force of many eyes tearing through him.

Chapter 80

His secretary buzzed him. "Ben, a Luis Armenta is on the phone. Should I take a message? I know that you're working on the Wilsons' demand letter."

"No, I'll take it."

"Hello, Ben Russo."

"I want to talk to you. In person. Today."

"Where? When?"

"A small lounge on Miracle Mile. The Green Dolphin. Not many people there during the week."

"I know the place. What time?"

"Six o'clock."

"I'll be there."

"Come alone. No tape recorder either. Can I trust you?"

"Yes, you can. See you later."

Luis looked at his watch fifty times before the meeting time arrived. Only a few patrons in the bar with separate scattered tables. One man had his hat on the table next to a half-filled bottle of Chivas Regal and two shot glasses. He looked up as Ben approached.

"I guess that you've been here for a while."

The man's eyes were narrow, red, and moist. "Drink, Senor, you've got a lot of catching up to do."

Several shots. Not a word spoken. Only the sound of poured scotch hitting the bottom of the glasses. The shorter man staggered to his feet and brought back another bottle from the bar.

"Luis, we can do this another time. Neither of us is ready to talk."

"No, Senor, it is now or never. I will have one more drink. The rest is yours."

"You know who I represent. There is no attorney-client privilege between us. I can go to the police with whatever you tell me. It is not confidential – you could go to prison."

Ben saw the tears rolling down the other man's cheeks. He felt uncomfortable, not worthy to be there. He wished that he were drunker.

"Come on, amigo, let's just drink. We can be serious next time."

Luis put both hands on his head. "I never intended this to happen. I can't live this way anymore. My insides are exploding. My wife does not even know. I've got to get it out—confessing to the priest was not enough." He stared at Ben. "I need to be punished. Listen to me."

He unloaded his guts. It was surreal. Ben wondered whether the encounter really happened. Only after shaking hands did it seem less mystical to him.

"Luis, I already told you that whatever you said would not be confidential. But one man to another, this conversation never happened unless I hear from you again. If I do not, any words spoken today would dry up like the rain in the hot desert sun. Do you understand? *Comprendes*?"

"*Comprendo*, amigo."

Ben prayed that night and asked the Lord to protect the soul of Luis Armenta.

"Please, God, let me do the right thing."

Regrettably, a few days later, he heard the words he most dreaded.

"Do what you have to do, *hombre*."

Chapter 81

He listened carefully to his lawyer.

"So, Raul, the murderer was this Cisneros guy. Probably now in Mexico. Maybe Hermosillo, according to Mr. Armenta. This could get complicated."

"What do you mean?"

"This Cisneros *hombre* is also a Mexican citizen. The Mexican government will not extradite their citizens back to the U.S. unless the prosecutor agrees to not seek the death penalty. Mexico does not execute anyone, no matter the crime. Cochise County will be forced to offer him a deal, a plea agreement."

"This animal killed my son and grandchild and will not be killed as punishment?"

"No…and the case against Luis Armenta is another matter. He was not the shooter and claims that he did not know that Cisneros was going to kill anyone."

"But you told me that he gave this *pendejo* money and where to find my son?"

"Yes, but—I'll go to the prosecutor. I don't trust the cops. They sometimes screw things up. They will arrest Mr. Armenta. How they deal with Cisneros— we'll see what happens. These things take time. You'll have to be patient."

The grieving eyes pierced Ben's soul. "Will my son get justice? My grandchild?"

The abogado touched the other man's shoulder. "I'll do whatever I can. Do you trust me, Senor?"

"*Si*, amigo, I trust you."

Chapter 82

6 August 2012, Tucson

Ben could not sleep. He regretted what he had orchestrated. He thought, "The animal who killed two people in cold blood gets twenty years and Luis could get ten years? He did not pull the trigger. Was not even there."

He felt compelled to do something he had never done before. Go behind a client's back. Do something without his permission or knowledge. It was probably unethical. But he could not help himself.

"Screw it. It's the right thing to do. Raul would never agree. The Bar can do whatever it wants. I'll be retired soon. I don't care."

His hand shook as he wrote.

Dear Judge Gomez:

As you know, I represent the family of the deceased, Jorge Verdugo. His father, Raul, hired me to investigate the death of his son. In the process of my representation, I interviewed Luis Armenta, the defendant and father of Frank Armenta, who died as a result of a car accident on 30 May 2010. Frank left a wife and two children.

It is my understanding that Luis Armenta will be sentenced on 13 August 2012, and faces between five and ten years in prison pursuant to a plea agreement. Probation is not available. Against my instincts as the legal representative of the Verdugo family members, and unbeknown to them, I write this letter. Hopefully, you will consider the contents in making your decision on sentencing.

Luis Armenta, without any concern for his future wellbeing and knowing that his statements would subject him to criminal prosecution, advised me of the following. He met Rafael Cisneros at the VFW hall and lamented over the death of his son. He told Mr. Cisneros that he thought that the Benson man who killed his son was not going to be justly punished. Mr. Cisneros told Mr.

Armenta that he could help and make things right by roughing up Jorge Verdugo. He would only use his fists and would stop when he drew blood. Mr. Armenta nodded and said twice that he did not want things to get out of hand and that absolutely no weapons of any kind could be used. Rafael agreed and then asked Mr. Armenta for a loan that he would repay. Luis took $200.00 cash out of his wallet and gave it to Mr. Cisneros, who immediately left. That was the only interaction between the two men.

For whatever it is worth, I totally believe the above account told to me. I have spent time in the presence of a seventy-year-old man tormented with guilt, regret, remorse, bewilderment, pain, and loss. He blames himself for what happened to Jorge Verdugo and Gloria Lopez. Some of that is valid. But the reality is that Luis Armenta had no idea that Mr. Cisneros would kill anyone as a result of that one conversation.

I have no standing or authority to recommend leniency in this matter. I realize that my client will despise me as a result of this letter. But this entire tragedy has given me many sleepless nights and regret my involvement.

I thank you for your time and patience.

Sincerely,
Ben Russo

Chapter 83

Sixty-year-old, Superior Court Judge Linda Gomez reread the pre-sentence report (PSR) and the Ben Russo letter. She momentarily paused and remembered her law school days thirty-five years ago. How fortunate she was that she had a roommate who took the sole blame for the marijuana found in their apartment. A neighbor complained about the noisy party. The police entered their humble abode and witnessed several law students getting high. Ruth Padia stepped up to the plate and glibly exonerated Linda of any knowledge or responsibility, reference the weed. Ruth was about to quit law school anyway and return to LA to marry her high school sweetheart. She knew that Linda had just been offered a job at a very prestigious, conservative law firm in Bisbee. The offer would evaporate if criminal charges were filed, even if jail time was not imposed.

The Judge thought, "Ruth was a great person. I can't do this today. I've studied this man in my courtroom. He does not belong in prison."

She asked her paralegal to tell the prosecutor and public defender to go to her chambers.

"Gentlemen, thanks for coming in. Sit down. Please listen carefully. What I am going to tell you will surprise you."

The prosecutor smirked. The young defense attorney slid low in his chair.

"I've read the PSR and the letter written by Ben Russo, which was unusual since he represents the Verdugo family. I'm also aware that co-defendant Rafael Cisneros is scheduled to be sentenced by Judge Martin in about a month. My understanding is that he will be extradited back to Arizona. Your office, Mr. Carpenter, stipulated a twenty-year sentence for the two murders. It appears that the defendant convinced someone that he was in fear of his life before killing the victims. Total nonsense, in my opinion, but it is not my problem."

The prosecutor leaned forward in his chair. "Your honor, in all due respect, my office had no choice, no control of the situation. The Mexican government refused to extradite unless the sentence was agreed to."

The Judge's face turned red. "Sir, let me tell you what I think. I accepted Mr. Armenta's plea agreement not knowing the circumstances of the case. A guilty plea to two murders as an accomplice? The factual basis for the plea was bogus from the beginning. The defendant had no knowledge that Gloria Lopez even existed. At best, he was guilty of solicitation to one count, and that is a stretch. I firmly believe that he did not know that Mr. Cisneros was going to kill or even seriously injure anyone. You have two choices. Take this case to another judge. I will not proceed with sentencing consistent with the plea agreement. I will not do it."

The prosecutor stood up. "Oh, come on, Judge. There are only three other criminal divisions. You are the presiding judge. No other division will accept this plea if you do not."

"Mr. Carpenter, here is your second choice. Prepare a plea agreement that designates the charge as soliciting the crime of manslaughter, one count, as it relates to Jorge Verdugo only. The sentencing range will be one to three years with credit for any time that the defendant has spent in county jail prior to sentencing. That is your only other option."

The prosecutor slapped the Judge's desk with both hands. "This is wrong! Two people were killed. You are not doing your judicial duty!"

The knuckles on the Judge's hands turned white. She stood up.

"Young man, if you defy me on this, your office will regret it dearly. I have a lot of discretion in ruling on motions, especially those based upon the fourth amendment in drug cases. I plan on being on the criminal bench for another ten years. Maybe I'll take a dimmer view of police searches and how they violate the constitutional rights of our citizens. I may even review some of my past rulings to see if I made any mistakes. Do you understand me?"

The prosecutor's shoulders slumped down as he silently sat down.

"Mr. Sinclair, do you object to anything I have said?"

The red-cheeked public defender managed a straight face. "No objection, your honor."

"Great. I'll see you both in one week, August 20th at 9 am."

Chapter 84

24 August 2012, Tucson

Late Friday afternoon. A tough week. Time to go home for the weekend and relax. Ben thought, "Only four months and one week to go. I can't freaking wait." He casually walked into the enclosed, mostly vacant parking lot and reached for his car keys. Something or someone emerged from behind one of the structural poles.

"You double-crossed me! You're a traitor! You helped the man who killed my son. Now I'm going to kill you!"

The light from the descending sun partially obscured the short, frail man holding a large pistol in both hands. The click of the hammer being pulled back broke the silence of the darkening space.

"No, Raul, don't do this! Let me explain."

The predator shortened the distance to his prey to within several feet. He lifted the deadly metal to shoulder level. His focused eyes were dark and deep. The larger man did not move. He stood with his hands at his sides.

A ray of diffused white light, an energy, entered the space between both men. The raised arms suddenly and uncontrollably shook and then froze. The heavy metal fell to the ground, making a loud clanking noise.

The smaller man put his hands over his anguished face and sobbed. The other man immediately approached and embraced the trembling figure before him. No words were spoken.

No one was ever told of this encounter. To the rest of the world, it never happened.

Chapter 85

24 December 2012, Tucson

Luis Armenta's taxi dropped him off. He knocked on the front door of the house. It was quiet, dark. He knocked again. Josie opened the door and smiled.

"*Mi amor.*"

He heard the music of mariachis getting louder and louder. He kissed his wife and stepped into the living room. Thirty-five family members and friends rushed in and shouted. "Feliz Navidad!"

He fell to his knees and cried.

Chapter 86

Ben looked at the sky and admired the heavenly stars. He thought, "What a beautiful night! I'm glad this legal shit is over. What a nightmare!"

He took a large swig of his third whiskey. He did not know whether he was Benedict Arnold or John the Baptist. Somehow the Tucson paper got wind of his role in the convoluted affair and printed several articles, all hyperbolic and cruel.

"Tucson attorney for victim helps murderer escape prison. What side was he on?"

He even received offers for the rights to his version of the story. Maybe even a book or movie deal. He turned to go back inside his quiet dark house. He noticed a small white dot, a sparkle of light above him, get larger and larger, closer and closer. It morphed into a transparent, blurry figure, human in shape, but with bumblebee-shaped wings. He whispered.

"Is that you, Dad?"

A strong deep voice emerged. "No, Ben. But we've been through a lot together…Brooklyn, Viet Nam. And here we are again. Who can forget the Berkmans? Scott says hello. Joy Tweet is doing great. I almost gave up on you, but the Lord persisted, as He always does."

Ben could see the vague outline of a face and mouth. "My time to return to Him has come. You are on your own from now on. You have been special to me. I'm here, to soothe your soul, give you peace of mind. Many people love you, miss you, want to share paradise with you for an eternity. Do not disappoint them. I pray that I will see you again. May God bless you always."

A sweet-smelling breeze brushed against Ben's face. The light ascended soon to be absorbed into the vast heavens above.

His neck and shoulders loosened. The weight and tightness subsided. Everything became clearer to him. He rushed to his bed, lay down, and gently touched the still arm of the woman he deeply loved. He smiled and kept his eyes open. He was no longer afraid of the dark.

Chapter 87

Ben Russo enjoyed his peaceful anti-social life spent mostly on his back porch. Retired for several years, approaching his eightieth birthday. He admired the birds, rabbits, squirrels, even coyotes, bobcats, javelinas on occasion. He read, watched TV, and played around on his personal computer.

The ringing of his cell phone startled him. Did he recognize the number? Should he answer it? Shit—Mario Grijalva. A lawyer in his mid-sixties. He clerked for Ben almost forty years ago. A friend. They went fishing and skiing in the White Mountains a few times. Even traveled together to Denver for a Broncos' game. They had not spoken for several years.

He picked up. "Hey, Ben, is that you? Mario Grijalva." His voice was high-pitched and squeaky.

"Oh, yeah, sure. You got me."

"Is everything OK? Can I talk to you for a minute?"

"Well, I guess—if you have to."

His cousin, Christopher Montano, was involved in a catastrophic accident. Two dead bodies. He represented Christopher. He needed help, guidance. In a tough spot.

"I wouldn't call, if I didn't need to."

"Well, why call me? I've been out of the loop for a long time."

Mario talked over him, interrupted him. "Ben, Ben, You've helped me in the past—please. I need a direction to follow. You always had great instincts."

"No, no. Get somebody still active—younger. I…"

"Come to the office. You still like Irish whiskey? Bushmill? Look at the file. Come on."

The anguish in the younger man's voice made a small dent in his armor.

"OK, OK. Mail a copy of what you have to my post office box. I'll call you—probably in a few days…"

It was almost 5 pm. Ben went to his refrigerator for a Bud Lite. He ran outside when he saw the white chested hawk perched on top of the telephone pole.

Chapter 88

The file was thick. Police reports, statements, drawings, medical records, photos of human destruction. He mumbled to himself. "Client does not remember anything? Traumatic brain injury? All eyewitnesses are cousins? Almost .02 alcohol content? He was driving? Sheriffs' department did a terrible job of investigation. Doesn't surprise me."

Ben placed paperwork in a drawer he never used. He did not want to see it—be reminded of it. He thought, 'I'll call him tomorrow—give him a few ideas—tell him to associate with a lawyer with personal injury experience—may need to hire an accident reconstructionist.

He poured his morning coffee and headed in the direction of the outside table. His wife Jennifer came in after her morning jog.

"What's up, Ben? You have that frown that I have not seen for years."

"Nothing important—I can handle it."

"Humor me—I have the time."

"You remember Mario? He wants me to help him on a case. Not interested. I'm content with my life."

"He's your friend...a nice guy. He taught the girls how to ski. Maybe it will do you some good to get out of the house—Get your brain moving again."

"What does that mean?"

"You spend all day waiting around for animals that never show up."

"Not true—I exercise, read a lot, do my chores, most of the cooking."

"Exercise? I watch you. You put on your sneakers, walk to the neighbor's house, and talk sports and politics, then you come back. Your decision. Do what you want, only my opinion."

She briskly walked away to her room for one hour of stretching and grunting.

He thought, "I'll sleep on it. I hate when she's right—which is most of the time."

Chapter 89

He tossed and turned all night. Old dreams returned. Walking on a mountain top—steep, slippery slopes over a one-thousand-foot cliff…can't find his homework…his classroom…rats are surrounding him…cannot move. He woke up. His undershirt was soaked. He quietly walked to the kitchen for a glass of water, sat down, and thought.

"It's too late. Back in the swamp. These dreams won't leave me unless I get it over with. Why did this asshole have to call me?"

Chapter 90

Mario quietly asked, "So you are going to help me? The clients are coming in tomorrow morning. Can you sit in? Maybe talk to them? Only if you want to."

Silence.

"A bottle of Bushmill will be waiting for you."

"Screw the bottle. What time?"

Chapter 91

The Crater on the left side of his head distracted Ben. Christopher Montano. Three months in intensive care at University Medical Center. Then airlifted to Barrows Neurological in Phoenix. In a coma for six weeks. Near death twice. The young man's eyes wandered around the room. His speech garbled. Saliva drooled from his mouth onto his chin. His wife dried it with a handkerchief. He was hard to understand.

Julie's sweet eyes studied his face as he tried for an hour to answer Mario's questions. How much did he drink before the accident? Who was there? What happened at the bar? What's the last thing that you remember? She leaned in to help. Then she glanced at his bewildered face and sat back. She did not want to embarrass or humiliate him.

Mario's bronze face drained to the color yellow. The athletic body drooped in his chair like spinach boiling in a pot. He turned to Ben. "Do you have any questions?"

Ben looked at her tired face. "Julie, do you have anything to add to what Christopher said?"

The young, beautiful Hispanic lady looked old, haggard. The space under her eyes was dark. The whites of her eyes were pink. She wore no makeup. Her clothes were too large for her petite body.

"Mr. Russo, Ben, I was not there. Know nothing about what happened. When I got to the hospital, Chris was in surgery. Later on, we never talked much about the accident. I just thank God that he is alive—I love him so much. We have two boys, six and four. If he goes to prison, what am I going to do?"

Her face crumbled to the table and stayed there. Ben was not ready for this. He was stuck in a marathon, and he could barely do the fifty-yard dash. He stared at the top of Julie's head and face immersed in a puddle of tears.

Mario looked up from his notepad. His hand shook when he put down his pen. "Let's take a break—ten minutes. Ben and I may have a few more questions. The bathroom is down the hall, on the left. Gloria can show you where it is."

The lawyers remained in the room alone. Mario faked a grin. "Ben, I know it's still morning, but do you want a beer? We'll pour it in a glass—Chris and Julie won't know."

The older man pondered the offer. "No, not today. I'll call you tomorrow—I'm sorry—just not myself today. I will give you my thoughts then." He hobbled to his feet.

"Wait up, amigo. Take this." Mario reached under the table and tried to hand him a large brown bag.

"Not today, Senor. Talk to you tomorrow." Ben walked through the inside door and waved to the young couple holding hands in the foyer.

Chapter 92

Ben waited two days. He drank a lot of his own booze to take the edge off life. He made the call to Mario who screamed into the phone.

"Hey, *viejo*, where have you been? I still have the whiskey here."

"Yeah, sure, great. I have a few ideas. Are you ready?"

"Help me, man. I'm all ears."

"Right. First the easy stuff. The two deceased young men, Peter and Manny, are thrown out of the truck onto the pavement. The police estimated that their bodies rolled fifty feet before they stopped on the left side of the road. The rolling caused massive injuries to their brains, according to the Medical Examiner. Chris' body was found thirty feet away but on the other side of the road. That's all the physical evidence the cops have."

Mario stopped taking notes and put the phone closer to his ear. "But, that's all they need, Senor. They have three witnesses saying that Chris was the driver. The blood tests at the hospital indicate that he was drunk—very drunk. What else is there?"

"Sure, but Marty, Johnny, and Frank are all related, first or second cousins."

"Is that a big deal?"

"Maybe—who knows? But ten minutes after the accident, Sergeant Davis approached them and asked them what happened. They looked at each other and said nothing. Just stayed quiet."

"Well, they were in shock—or they did not want to snitch on their friend Chris."

"Could be, but, and don't take this the wrong way, Mexicans make a big deal out of being related to someone, even if he is a dick. One of these guys would have said that Chris was driving if he just killed their cousins. Anyway, the cop never pushed. He should have separated them. He did not do his job."

"Ben, Davis could have got spooked. He had just seen Chris' squashed head dripping from the rock he plowed into. He's only human."

"A lot of maybe this, maybe that. Make sure all these guys are separated when you interview them."

"This is all basic shit, amigo. Tell me what I don't know. I've known you a long time. You always seemed to pull something out of that chunky ass of yours." He laughed long and hard at his own joke.

"Thanks for the compliment, puto. Try to listen. Many years ago, a Tucson lawyer got a huge personal injury victory at trial. The Trial Reporter said he retained a PhD. Engineer. There was an issue of negligence. In other words, why did the accident happen? I heard through the grapevine that the expert was incredible."

"But that was a civil case where the fault was contested. Do we have that here? Three witnesses plus a high blood alcohol reading. That's manslaughter. A minimum of twelve years."

"You missed the main point. A criminal case—reasonable doubt. Let's see if we can create that. It's not our job to prove who was driving. Only that maybe Chris wasn't."

"Good luck. Get back to me when you know something useful. Keep your time. I will pay you, eventually."

"Sure you will, *mentiroso*."

Chapter 93

Ben futilely wracked his flabby brain. "What the hell was the name of the lawyer who hired the egghead engineer?"

He called Mario's secretary and asked her to bring him the Pima County Bar directory. She lived close by. He figured that the attorney, younger than himself, probably still practiced. He thought, "These rich elitists never retire. They die in their leather chairs behind their mahogany desks. They're addicted to money and adulation."

Jim Warren was pleasant, even cordial, on the phone. He had two clients on hold. Once he found out that it was a criminal case, the call ended. Ben wasted no time.

"Hello, is Dr. Stan Bloom available?"

"Who is calling? Are you a salesman? Dr. Bloom is in a meeting."

"No, no, I am a Tucson lawyer, a retired one. I want to hire Dr. Bloom reference an accident. I need…"

The other voice talked over him. "Dr. Bloom will call you back. I have another call waiting. What's your name and phone number?"

It seemed like eternity to Ben, but it was actually only a week. Dr. Bloom, PhD, a graduate of MIT, Harvey Mudd, and Caltech, was on the line. The human computer did not want to chat or go down memory lane. He cut Ben off in mid-sentence.

"Send me what you have. I'll get back to you in a week, maybe two. Got to run."

Nothing for ten days. Ben dialed the doctor's number several times but hung up after the first ring. He hated dead time. Mario's frenzied calls gave him indigestion. On the fourteenth day, he saw the number he was waiting for.

"Ben, Stan Bloom. Do you have a few minutes?"

"Sure, sure, doctor."

"Call me Stan. Two quick questions. You represent Mr. Montano, one of the survivors, is that correct?"

"Yes. We sent you photos of his head taken at the hospital. He's still suffering from traumatic brain injury."

"OK. This is a criminal case. Right?"

Ben breathed hard. He expected a polite rejection. "Yes, sir."

"You need to show reasonable doubt which would result in a not guilty verdict? Correct?"

"Exactly, Doctor—I mean Stan."

"This is not what I usually do. But this case intrigues me—challenges me to stretch, expand. I can help you. This is what I need before I spend any more time on this."

Ben summarized his conversation with the good doctor. Mario acted like a dog licking his master when he came home. The fees would be substantial, but the rewards potentially awesome.

"Mario, you will be on the hook to pay a shit load of money to this guy. Can you swing it? Will your clients reimburse you?"

He responded in a heartbeat. "We have no choice. The family will help. They love Chris. The local Guard has already started a collection for attorney's fees. I've got money saved up for a boat. Fuck the boat."

Chapter 94

Ben spoke in Mario's office three weeks later. "Boy, these M.I.T guys. Will the jury understand this shit? The report said that all his findings and conclusions will be presented by PowerPoint?"

Mario shrugged his shoulders as he ate a grilled cheese sandwich. "I have no clue. Does the Court have that technology?"

"Who knows? It's freaking fantastic that he concludes that Chris could not have been the driver. But one thing really bothers me. Bloom seems to imply that Manny, one of the dead guys, was the driver. Do you read it that way?"

"I'll have to look at it again. But so what? Who cares?"

"Mario, we have to be very careful. The decedent cannot defend himself. The grieving family will be in the courtroom. Will the jury hate us if we present that? Anyway, we'll deal with it later on down the road." Ben stared at the wall, stood up, and walked toward the door.

"Ben, stay a while. Let's have a drink. It's early. What do you want?"

"Not in the mood. Send a copy of the report to the prosecutor. Set up the interviews of the three guys and the cop. The prosecutor will call you in a few days to tell you that Bloom's report is bullshit. Don't let him spook you. Politely listen. He'll advise you that he's hired his own expert who will blow the good doctor out of the water. Don't be cocky. I'll call you on Monday. Have a good weekend."

"Come on, amigo. Stay with me for a drink. Look—Johnnie Walker Black. Good stuff. I just bought it."

"Save your money. By the end of the trial, you'll be in debt for mucho dinero."

"Not your problem, *viejo*."

"One more thing—I'm only going to be involved with the interviews of the experts. Just tape the other ones. I'll review them after they have been transcribed."

Mario took the cork off the bottle and frowned. "Are you baling on me already? What's going on?"

"I'm not your babysitter. I'll be spending a lot of time preparing the questions for Bloom and their expert. You need me on that. In all due respect, my friend, you will fuck that up without my help. And then, hasta la vista, baby. God forbid that happens. One way or another, Chris will die in prison before his time is up."

Ben briskly exited and ignored the droning in the background.

Chapter 95

Every night, for two weeks leading up to the trial—scary, complicated, weird dreams. Ben opened his eyes in the dark and prayed. "Dear God, give Mario the wisdom and strength to do it."

Mario sat behind his desk and nodded in the way that always annoyed the older man.

"Got it. We'll do fine. Get some sleep tonight. You look like shit. Try to look presentable tomorrow. What size suit do you wear? My chubby uncle is about your size."

"Screw you. Remember, don't get cute with any witnesses. Keep your ego in check. No peacocking during the trial. I printed out the questions for the experts. I don't have a suit that fits me. I have a few sports jackets and some decent dress pants. Take it or leave it. My ties are pretty good. Red for power. Blue for truthfulness."

Chapter 96

The courtroom was packed when they walked in. Ben heard his footsteps as they approached the defense table. Mario started to sit in the chair on the left side. Ben talked softly.

"No. Sit on the right side. I'll sit in the middle. You want the jury to see Chris' head."

The distraught extended families sat on the prosecutor's side. Chris, Julie, frightened family members and friends, and several National Guard soldiers in their dress uniforms on the other side. It took an entire day to pick the jury. The pool was diverse. Many said anything to get out of serving. A few were eager to get picked. Ben's blue-collar childhood, Army experience, and hundreds of trials gave him instincts many others did not have. He did not care what someone said in the presence of others. What was in their heads? Is the woman's smile real? Why does that guy stare at Chris and then look at his watch? Will the old janitor understand the expert testimony? Who will be the leaders of this group of strangers? What side will they be on, at least in the beginning?

The jury pool left along with most of the spectators on both sides. A few never left the room. Ben turned to his right and glanced at a very well-dressed Hispanic lady, probably in her sixties. She immediately looked away. Her eyes were unusually dark and large. He noticed that she held a rosary in one hand and a book in the other.

This was the one process that he had long mastered. Very few were better. He took over. Mario only nodded at his picks. He liked teachers and nurses. They were kind, thoughtful, and empathetic. Police officers, security guards, wanna be cops? No. Eggheads? Probably, but only in this case. Educated? Yes. Mexicans? Not so much. Asians? No way. Who served on a criminal jury before? What was the verdict?

Seven women and five men. One teacher. Two nurses. Several blue-collar guys. An Asian chemist. A mixture of Anglos and Mexicans. A black doctor. Ben laughed to himself.

"An African-American physician in Tucson? Where did he come from?"

The first week went quickly, smoothly. No surprises. Some hills, valleys, small victories, and defeats. The three cousins stuck to their stories. Even tried to shed some tears. The jury paid very close attention to the Medical Examiner's testimony concerning the cause of death of the two young men. The prosecutor surprised Ben when he offered the gruesome photos of Chris' head into evidence. They could not object. It was in their list of exhibits. Ben thought, "Smart move. He wants the jury to minimize their importance."

The prosecutor asked leave to approach the bench. He spoke very softly. "Your honor, before the State rests, I need to discuss a legal matter. It may be better to do this without the jury being present."

The Court agreed.

"OK, the jury is not here. Has the State finished presenting its case?"

"The defense has advised us that it will call an expert witness to the stand. If it does, the State has an expert in rebuttal. With that on the record, the State rests."

The Judge looked at Mario. "Mr. Grijalva, has the defendant decided whether or not he will testify?"

"He will not, your honor."

"Well, it is 11:15. Call your expert, and we will break for lunch at noon."

Mario's face turned white. He and Ben had anticipated that the State would call a few additional witnesses. He began to stutter. Ben jerked on his arm.

"Your honor, could I have a minute to confer with my assistant, Mr. Russo?"

"Make it quick, counselor."

Ben talked fast. "Bloom won't be here until 12:15. Ask the Judge to break for lunch now, then come back early."

Mario's eyes glazed up.

"Do it—do it—be polite. Tell him that Bloom is on the way."

The Judge listened. He did not know Mario. He recognized Ben and remembered that he never acted like a hemorrhoid in his courtroom. He looked at the prosecutor and expected a strong objection. But it never came. Only a shrug of the shoulders. Ben was not surprised. Bloom had been annoyingly condescending during the State's interview. The prosecutor thought that Bloom was a pompous elitist. He looked forward to tearing him a new asshole.

"OK, we start promptly at 12:45. If the expert is not here then, we begin closing arguments."

Ben had to pee three times in the next hour. His stomach ached and bloated until Bloom arrived at 12:35. He now felt that Angelina Jolie had begged him to go to bed with her. The good doctor smiled.

"Traffic was bad—sorry for that. Is there a bathroom close by?"

The two lawyers simultaneously responded.

"Hurry."

Ben glanced at the script, the list of witnesses to be asked. He touched Mario's shoulder.

"Don't freelance or go rogue."

The doctor humbly and thoroughly responded to all of Mario's questions. His assistant, an intense young lady, a doctoral candidate, skillfully maneuvered the intricacies of the PowerPoint presentation. She was the orchestra. Bloom was the maestro waving his wand directing all the various parts.

Ben thought, "This guy is something else. I even believe him."

Everything asked and answered. Nothing further to do. At least that's what was in Ben's mind. He saw Mario start to rise from his chair with his smart-alecky look. Was he going to ask more questions? Ben grabbed the back of his suit jacket. He pulled hard. He whispered. "You're done. Stay in your chair."

The younger and stronger man tried again to escape. Ben now used both of his hands. Finally, the light bulb turned on.

"No more questions, doctor. Thank you for your testimony."

The prosecutor had no choice. He had to take the only path available to him. The engineer's credentials were impeccable. His findings and conclusions made sense. His own expert once worked for the good doctor and secretly revered him. He had to get the jury to dislike the brilliant man. Convince them to ignore, not care what he said, even if true. Jury nullification. Like what Johnny Cochran did to the LA police. He owed it to the victims and their families. They needed something good to come out of this trial.

"Dr. Bloom, you live and work in Scottsdale, is that correct? You don't spend too much time in Tucson, do you? You went to all private colleges for your degrees—in Boston, Los Angeles—is that right? Have you ever served your country? Ever been in the military?"

He turned around and faced the soldiers. "Have you ever spoken to the family members of the two young men who died as a result of this accident? Ever shared their grief?" He pirouetted to his rear. "Your report accuses the decedent, Manny Montenegro of causing his own death and that of his cousin, Peter Padia?" He put his head down and shook his head.

"A good young man who cannot defend himself today. The defendant's blood alcohol content was more than twice the legal limit. I'm sure you are aware of that? That fact, not fiction, is hidden away somewhere in your report. You go even further, sir. You are telling this jury that three other victims of this horrible, preventable tragedy lied to the jury. For some unknown reason, committed perjury. Is that what you are saying? Do you have children, doctor? Have you any idea what it is like to have a child die? Your whole career, and most of your income, is based upon enabling wealthy attorneys to get even richer in car accident cases, is that accurate?" He glared at Mario. "By the way, how much money is Mr. Grijalva paying you for your report and testimony?" He picked up the report and tossed it under the table.

Mario wanted to make many objections to the questions. Some were valid. Ben held him back. The jury heard it. Be stoic. Don't make it worse. The doctor was bruised but was still standing. He was used to being grilled over the coals by incredibly talented insurance defense attorneys, trying to save their clients millions of dollars. The prosecutor, at least to the good doctor, was merely an annoyance, like a fly on your hamburger, a mosquito landing on your arm. Nothing deadly.

Ben conceded in his own mind that the cross-examination was effective. The State had a fighting chance. The prosecutor should have rested his case. But he made the decision, motivated mostly by his ego, to call his expert. Many of the points he had skillfully made, lost their importance. Bloom compared to Paul Cline was Marilyn Monroe compared to Olive Oyl. George Clooney versus the Elephant Man.

The jury was out for two days. Ben was home when he got the call. He very tightly grabbed the steering wheel of his twelve-year-old Honda. His hands hurt when he took the key out of the ignition. He felt dizzy when he walked up the flight of stairs of the courthouse. He stared at the jurors as they walked into the eerily silent room. The jurors sat and kept their eyes fixated on the table before them. He saw some papers in the older lady's hand. The school teacher. Maybe the jury foreperson? A good sign. She smiled at him once during the trial. Not bad looking. Her teeth looked like they had been chemically bleached to the color of ivory.

The Judge came in. All stood up. "Has the jury reached verdicts on both counts of the indictment? If so, will the jury foreperson please stand up and read the verdicts?"

The tall black doctor stood up. Ben's heart sunk to his feet. He internally lamented.

"Educated blacks are usually conservative. Two dead bodies. We're screwed."

The man's voice was powerful and clear. "Count one—Not Guilty. Count two—Not Guilty."

Julie bolted up and placed her wobbly head on her husband's shoulder. Chris did not move from his chair for several seconds. He then slowly stood up, placed his arms around his wife's shaking torso, and stared at the ceiling fan above him.

Ben had seen enough. He could not stop the river from overflowing its banks. He sobbed but stopped when he realized that people were looking at him. He did not want to be part of the noise, crying, happiness, anger, disappointment, grief, shock, sadness, and euphoria surrounding him. He picked up his file, ignored anyone who tried to speak to him, hurriedly walked out of the building, and drove home way above the speed limit. He did not listen to his wife's questions and jumped on his bed with all his clothes on. He missed dinner and slept until morning.

Chapter 97

His phone rang for several days. He never picked up. Jennifer touched his shoulders and put her face very close to his.

"Ben, call Mario. I am sure that the calls are from him. They are very annoying."

He obeyed. Mario answered.

"Are you all right? You looked pretty shook up after the verdicts."

"I'm fine. But that was my last curtain call. No more."

"I have a few presents for you. Jameson's and some Scotch made off the coast of England. I'm not going to tell you how much it cost me. Don't slug it down like you do Bud Lite."

"You didn't have to do that."

"Are you kidding me? You saved my cousin's ass. Come in tomorrow. We'll celebrate."

Chapter 98

Ben parked at 4 pm. He did not want to get there too early. He would get too drunk. A car passed by, made an illegal U-turn, and stopped near the curb a half block down the street. He mumbled.

"Shitty driver."

Two sixteen-ounce beers later and countless insults, bad jokes, and put-downs, it was 5 pm.

"Time for me to go, Mario. The old lady is cooking tonight. 5:30 sharp. She gets nasty when I'm late."

"OK. *Viejo*. I won't push you today. Don't forget the booze."

Mario had already passed through the inside door leading to the foyer. Ben was a few feet behind when he thought that he heard firecrackers. Blood and parts of Mario's head exploded into his face and onto his shirt. He watched his friend slowly crumble to the cement and land with a thump. He looked up. Dark, black, evil eyes. Then a high-pitched voice.

"You're next, motherfucker! This is from Manny, my godson."

The first bullet penetrated his left lung. The second tore away his throat. He spun to the left, hitting the wall. The bottles crashed to the ground. His body crushed the broken glass next to his comrade. He could not breathe or talk. His eyes remained open. A light slowly descended, getting brighter and brighter. Then a different voice.

"Your time has come, my friend. He is waiting—for both of you."

The light dissipated from view. The drowning mouth slightly opened. The eyes momentarily looked up and then shut. The life-giving liquid oozed from the cadavers and merged into one indivisible puddle. By the time earthly death was discovered, a heavenly orchestrated sunrise had already emerged, foreordaining eternal peace and love for those souls worthy of paradise.

Epilogue

Hundreds of people gathered to mourn Ben's death. Several actually loved him. Most just knew him, liked him, and wanted to show their regrets for his untimely and unforeseen death. Julie and Chris were there with the boys.

Three years later, Jennifer married a younger more vigorous man, with whom she had more in common, and who participated in the activities of her life. She did not love this man, as she did Ben, but he was pleasant, fun to be with and enthusiastically satisfied all of her needs. The two daughters accepted this man, not as their father, but as an affable partner to their energetic mother.

Ben's story is just one example of life's wonders. Whether one believes in a God, an energy, a spiritual power that orchestrates the world, is not important. Forces of love and generosity exist in everyone's life, whether one is rich, poor, handsome, beautiful, ugly, deformed, old, young, smart, dumb, or a combination thereof. They may not be as dramatic as a bright light or a mystical voice.

Someone patting you on the back after you struck out with the bases loaded in a Little League game. Who tells you that you will do better next time, that you are really good, and that you should not give up. The teacher who goes out of his way to help you succeed in math in high school. The older lady who smiles and holds the door for you when your hands are stuffed with children and groceries. A friend who listens to you, addresses, and fights your demons, tells you that there is nothing to worry about, that things will get better, and that tomorrow is only a day away. These guardian angels are eager to help carry the weight of the cross burdening your weary shoulders and soften your falls from the tightrope of life.

Ben knew that he had a Wing Man. Most humans do not. But all souls are aware of His existence.